'Another winner. . . . The world is one colossal city, built even over the oceans. Decayed humanity is dependent on the Machines – but who controls the Machines, and why? A remarkable effort of sustained imagination' – *Methodist Recorder*

'Vincent King's imaginative powers are well-served by his talent for writing. . . . The succession of events leading to the climax is a tour de force' – *Scotsman*

'Bizarre fantasy, with more illusions than hall of mirrors. Oddball, central character weaves his way through weirdly rotten city of the future, and some nasty encounters, to final truth. Alpha all along the line' – *Birmingham Evening Mail*

Candy Man

VINCENT KING

SPHERE BOOKS LIMITED
30/32 Gray's Inn Road, London WC1X 8JL

First published in Great Britain by Victor Gollancz Ltd 1971
Copyright © Vincent King 1971

First Sphere Books edition 1973

TRADE
MARK

Set in Times Roman

Printed in Great Britain by
Hazell Watson & Viney Ltd
Aylesbury, Bucks

ISBN 0 7221 5264 7

CHAPTER ONE

THE LAST FINGERNAIL of moon set through the shaggy branches. Midnight went by, hours passed onwards, I lay lonely. Like always . . . like I always seemed to, the way I always liked to.

It was a high and sad place up in the lichen woods. Lonely, like my mind. I went up there sometimes when I got afraid of myself.

So then it started raining. I felt myself get cold. When I noticed the rain freezing on my rubbers I came down out of there. I'd run out of tubes; anyway I had what I wanted . . . it was time to come down. I didn't like it on the Streets, but you couldn't live for ever in the woods. My dog didn't like it up there either. Man . . . but it was lonely!

All that pale green-grey . . . that crumbly lichen, rubbery and crumbly . . . exquisite convolutions, beautiful like brains . . . but so *strange*. No man's place, not *right*. I didn't remember exactly, but I knew things should have been better . . . it was like those big words I used sometimes, it was like a memory that somehow wasn't mine. Maybe it was just that someone told me about good things.

That lichen grew on the trees, sucked them dry, shrivelled them brittle . . . like it would your brain if you let your mind start thinking about it. It was odd . . . something alien . . . something *else* . . . and sometimes I felt like that too.

All the broken walls there, the twisted Concrete . . . bent and bubbled, poking up from the thin soil. But somehow you only saw things ugly when you were coming down. It was all beautiful when I was tired of the world and on the way up. Maybe it's that you can't see things you don't want to look at.

As I said, I had what I went for. I whistled my dog

and started towards where I could see the valley floor looking like grey ash under the thin snow. Farther on the trees ended and the mud was crusted with frost, thawing a little in the rain. I crouched and took a long look ahead. You never knew. You had to be careful when you didn't have a name. You didn't want to meet any unexpected Teachers and have them asking questions.

What I minded most was not having a name. Not a real one, I mean. It's like not having a shadow. It's a bad feeling . . . it was as if you weren't complete . . . not really a man, a freak. It was as if you were really bad luck . . . not a part, always outside.

If you missed the Rites, when they gave them out, you just didn't get a name at all . . . and then after a while they were after you and you had to keep hid. That's why I was where I was, that's why I had to go to the woods. Some of the young ones respected me for it—before they went to the Rites, failed and got their brains burned. My dog didn't have a name either, but sometimes I called him Wolf.

You missed the Corps tests, too, that's what the Rites were really, but I didn't mind that so much. They shouldn't have made men go without a name. Maybe, I thought, maybe I'll make them give me mine one day. It wasn't right. I wished the Saver would come, like someone prophesied once. Someday someone would get up and put it all right, give me my name, everything, and he'd be the Saver. Maybe he'd be something to do with Exploration Corps, when the big ships came back from the Stars, from wherever it was they were supposed to be. Nobody knew when he'd come . . . or what he'd do. If I'd known that then I'd have done it and been him. I wondered who. I wondered who it would be. I wondered what it was all for, what was the Purpose, what I was alive for. I wished I had a name.

I ignored the first couple of places down there. Too small. I didn't like to be obvious. I stayed up a few yards under the treeline, looked down into each soggy, misty vale and went on to the next. You could keep hidden in the big places, keep hidden and do good business. I hitched up my tray and bucket and went on. Anyway, there were thirty or forty lights in the next one so I went down there. After some scrabbling and climbing I made it to the first houses.

There was a dark place at the top of the Street under the gantry so I stood looking and listening. I hadn't been in that place before. I was coming from up the line, from the north, like they said up there.

I checked how my machine worked and the loads in the powder guns the Teachers gave me. I made sure the wheels were free, checked the pyrites and set the springs. Then the Boy came out of the shadows and looked at me. Wolf growled once to tell me he was a stranger; after a while, when nothing happened, I thought it'd be OK.

I wasn't sure if the Boy had seen what I was doing, so I ignored him. He didn't say anything, he just stood there, sizing me up.

I adjusted the bandage on my eyes. It was made of funny stuff, you could see right through it from one side. It was from the old days, or maybe it was from the Corps. I found a woman's dress made of it and used what was still good to make a bandage. Anyway, I wore it over my eyes and people thought I was blind. It gave me an edge, and I never wanted to see the world too clearly.

I pulled the thing farther down over my cheeks and all the time the Boy was watching me and smiling with his full lips. After a while he went away, but I still didn't know if he'd seen the powder guns inside my tray.

In the end I decided he hadn't and that there wasn't anything to wait for. I swung down the Street for where people ought to be.

The canteen was the usual place. Noisy and hot and dark. All the usual loud music beating and synthetic in the Speakers. People seemed to like it in the dark. They all lay about and didn't move much. I struck sparks to the wicks of the spirit lamps and pretty soon the machine was hot enough. I spun the flywheel, spilled in sugar and some of the crushed beetles and flies to give it colour. I started making candyfloss.

"Hey . . . Candy Man . . . !" Some of the women started to get up.

"Sweet Candy!" They always liked me, called me Candy

Man until they knew me better. "Good sweet Candy Man is here!"

Not long and everybody was eating my floss and paying me too. Nobody cheated me. It was bad Luck to cheat a blind man. Like disobeying a Teacher. It was grained deep, like religion, like that yarn about the Saver. The women always saw me first, they were least stupid.

I watched the childish faces. None of them had dodged the Rites . . . they all had their names. Bastards! I made myself hate them, all of them had the forehead scars. I had a scar myself, but I put it there. I didn't get it at any Rites, that's why they called me Candy Man, but it wasn't the same as a name, not my *name* . . . not *really*.

When they were all served, while I waited for the floss to take, I stood with my head up like a blind man and took in the rest of the crowd. There were a couple of other blind men, sometimes the Rites go wrong, that's how you got blind. That's why they call it Lucky. Like not to discourage people from the Rites. Over by the door that Boy was stood, picking his teeth and moving his lips.

Time went on and I watched the people closer. Their eyes had that glazed look I hated so, that look that went with having a name. You could tell from their talk how they were. The women weren't developed properly either. Little pimple breasts. You could see they'd never had kids and most of them never would. Their shirts were open to their navels, they didn't care, or maybe it was some fashion they'd got a hold of.

Some of them were starting to sweat. The black stuff was running down their faces and making runnels between their narrow bosoms. It seemed to wash them a little cleaner in places. I didn't like them much. I mean, what's it all for? What were we all for? I started preaching then. I always waited until the women started sweating. It wasn't only cochineal in my floss—you had to do something to liven them up.

"HEAR THE VOICE OF LUCKY BLIND SWEET CANDY MAN OUT OF THE WILDERNESS, WOODS AND HIGH PLACES!" I saw the Boy had come forward into the light to watch me better. He stood just behind the people, listening hard. He certainly stood out. The way he was grinning. His clothes too, so *clean*. Velvet knee breeches, a white blouse thing with ruffles down the front and at the cuffs . . . buckled shoes. I went right on preaching and soon forgot him.

"I DRINK DEEP IN THE LICHEN POOLS . . . FIND YOU THE COLOURED BEETLES IN THE CACTUS JUNGLES! I HAVE SEEN THE HIGH SIGHTS, THE GLORIES AND THE REVELATIONS!" I had to yell at first but when they started to listen I dropped my voice right down and they had to cluster close to hear. So they had to concentrate on what I said. I worked hard at it, and all the time I was wondering who was really being fooled.

"Now listen. You know the sin of sucking devil's juices from the Dispensers, you know it! You *know* it—and you still live by it! Our mothers told us, our fathers told us too . . .

"When our ancestors . . . our fathers . . . when they came out from the deeps of slavery and the thrall and bondage of our history, in those days that the hand of the Saver was with us—when we were provided for—was that done so we could suckle on the hell emissions of the easy Dispensers?" I could see the ranked nozzles in the background. They were well used, the thick chrome mostly worn off. One or two dripped, pools of nutrient lay there. What a way to treat people, what a way to feed them!

"Forbidden! FORBIDDEN! Remember that the lights are going to be the sky again! How will the Saver come when you feed on evil? When you batten on the work of the Great Robot?" All of them were listening to me. It only took a mention of 'Ancestors', a word of the Saver and a scream or two about the Great Robot that the Teachers told us was coming to end the world if we didn't behave ourselves, and they'd follow you anywhere. Throw in a few words they didn't understand and they'd eat off your floor too. All the old magic myths, they'd believe anything. I began to feel really Lucky. I used to try not to care too much about old things I half remembered. I tried to concentrate on today and tomorrow . . . mostly on to-day . . . how it went and what it was for.

"DOWN ON YOUR KNEES!" The floss had really started to bite by then. Jaws sagged, the women swayed to the rhythms of my talking. I started to beat my tray like a

9

drum. Pretty soon they all took it up and then it was easy

That time I was feeling really *Lucky*. I pretended to grope over to the table. I climbed up on it and stood there yelling.

"SAVER'S COMING!"

"YES! IT'S PROMISED!" They shouted back at me.

"AND THE STARS ARE GOING TO SHINE!" Saver might know what that meant. They shone every night, unless it rained.

"Yes! They're going to *shine*!"

" THEY WILL . . . ! I SURELY KNOW THEY WILL!" They were really going. Hips and bellies thrusting out to the beat of it . . . all to my rhythm. It never took much. Just some of that stuff you squeeze out of those certain flies, that and a little repetition. I slipped in another reference to the Great Robot just to hear them scream and went on about myself.

"I'M BLIND, BROTHERS! I may look like I'm a crazy blind man but I sure see right from wrong!" I'd started shouting again and I hadn't meant to. I was *Lucky*, I really believe I was Lucky then. I could feel the *power*. I *knew* I was something special and I really had *Purpose*. The people . . . I had them right there with me. We were each other and we were all together. It should have been like that all the time . . . But I had to get my tubes. I always had to get my tubes.

"AND I SEE THE RITES! The *Rites*, brothers . . . they put the evil in us *then*!"

"Evil . . . ? Rites . . . ?" It was hard for them. The Teachers always told them the evil was taken *out* then. I saw the Boy still watching. He hadn't had floss, his mouth was open and he was listening to me.

"THE SCARS! It's what makes the scars! You can't put bad Luck in without making scars! If they took it out we'd heal clean! There'd be no scars then!" The Boy laughed, but he nodded his head with the rest of them. I didn't care what he thought, standing there in his fancy clothes. Right then it came!

"EVIL!" It was one of the men, screaming. "Evil . . . the Rites are *evil*!" His voice trailed off. Maybe he realised what he'd said.

I pulled one of the guns out of my tray, aimed, broke one of his legs for him by hitting it just right. I turned and made for the Speaker. I suppose I felt bad about it, but I'd done it before and I knew I'd do it again. It wasn't as if I'd *killed* him.

A woman with spittle on her chin grabbed me round my rubbery legs. I kicked her off. She didn't care. I hated it all, but I still went to the Speaker.

"Kids," said someone. "Got to stop them. . . stop them from the Rites . . . stop them being like us!" They were slow, but that was the idea. Maybe they were catching on. I looked for legs to break but I couldn't see in the crowd. Anyway, one was enough.

I made it to the Speaker, hit the call button. The Boy was watching me, smiling, a sort of fascinated horror on his face. Maybe I'd have broken his legs too, but then he slipped away. The urgency for tubes was on me, I could have done anything then.

The Speaker answered. There wasn't any picture on the screen. It'd only have been the Machine . . . anyway, it would have been watching.

"Yes?" is said. *"Name?"*

"A man here," I said quickly. "A man here said the Rites were *evil*, said we shouldn't send the children!" There was a pause while the recall got checked. They can't watch everyone all the time, but they can record it.

"Thank you. Confirmed." The voice was quite toneless, my tubes clicked out into the reward tray. I always liked the sound of the Machine's voice . . . it sounded like home, maybe it was the tubes it gave me.

Anyway, it was time to go. I began to elbow back across the room. I looked up and saw the Boy, he was really laughing by then. At what I did, I suppose. But hell, I had to have my tubes!

I kicked a woman off me again. She rolled on the floor. Ecstasy, I thought, or maybe I really hurt her. I couldn't tell, but I was glad I had my rubbers and she couldn't touch me.

They were copulating everywhere. On the floor, on the stairs, there was even a couple out on the Street. I never understood how they could do it like that. They were

11

moaning and turning, grunting like pigs. I shouted over it, I still had something to say.

"SO I'M GOING TO TELL YOU, BROTHERS AND SISTERS!"

"Yes . . . yes . . ." Someone answered, maybe the rest could hear me.

"You let *love* in! YOU LET OLD LOVE GET INTO YOU!" Love . . . I didn't see how you could call it that. I never understood about that . . . "YOU MAKE LOVE, BROTHERS AND SISTERS . . . you make love and children!" I was nearly at the door. It was what I meant, it was what I had to say.

It was what I had my power for, right then I was sure it was my Purpose. Mostly, after the Rites, they were too stupid to breed even. Maybe there was something they put in the nutrient too, I knew some got sterilised at the Rites. So I did what I could to put that right with my preaching and my floss. Maybe they were trying to wipe out the human race . . . kill us all by slow degrees. If I could make people love and breed, then there'd be more people to go on. Maybe they wouldn't all go to the Rites, not if I could preach enough. If the Teachers kept on oppressing them maybe the people would even revolt. There were several ways I might win, the race might win, but anyway there always had to be people. That's what I was trying to do, that and getting my tubes. I didn't see how one man could do enough, but I had to stay outside and try. Maybe, I used to think, maybe it was my Purpose, maybe it was what I was for . . . and maybe it was worth the way I did it.

A man came at me so I clobbered him with the gun and he went down OK. When they came out of the Rites they stopped growing so they were easy, that was why the Boy didn't look small amongst them.

GO NOW!" I shouted back from the door. "Leave it! DON'T SIN ANY MORE! Love each other . . . !" They got to it and I stepped out. The Boy was over across the Street and he nearly fell over laughing when I said that. All I thought was that it was taking too long. I should have been gone. That was when the Whistler came.

I heard it first. I was listening for it. I always was.

A puff of air from far below. The quick throb of pressure change. A little sound, getting louder. I started to move and the Boy heard it too. I began to run around the pavement. I got ten paces and the Whistler arrived. They were *quick*, that's why they worried me so.

That great shining screw disc came twisting and biting up its slots, pushing itself hard up behind the air blast, sealing the Street as it came.

I was too late, so was the Boy. We turned like one man back into the canteen to try and get out farther down.

The Boy tagged behind. I tripped and fell amongst the people. I got up quickly and looked back. The Whistler opened like an egg. The Teacher came out all in one smooth movement.

He looked straight at us across the slow pulsing bodies. Everybody else ignored him. They were far away, they were lucky.

Those steel hard eyes, set in that grey metal mask with the flush rivets and the lacing up the middle. That terrible metal face you could see yourself reflected in it.

"YOU!" he screamed. "YOU STAND STILL!"

Those weapons. They were worse than ever. Those blunt metal cylinders poking out of the chair arms, those things traversing slowly across the room. Hell, he didn't really need them. He was a *Teacher*.

"Stand still while I am talking to you!" There was a long silence while he looked the room over. You wouldn't think so much death could come out of those blank metal ends.

"A report," he said at last. "Someone hates the Rites. Someone thinks that they are *evil*. You?" The Boy sniggered. All the time he was picking his teeth. I'd never seen anything like that in front of a Teacher.

"Him!" I jerked my thumb at the Boy. He should laugh.

"Your name?"

"WADZ B(869)," the Boy spoke seriously. The Teacher punched some buttons on the arm of his chair. There was a chattering and clicking as it went down to the Deep Machine to be written down.

"We will remember you for the Rites." The Teacher turned to me. "Name?"

13

"Candy man . . ." My throat clicked. It came out before I could stop it. It was all I could say. "They call me Sweet Candy Man . . ."

The Teacher wheeled forward. Fixed me with those horror eyes. One of the weapons came out and poked me in the chest.

"NAME?" He sounded puzzled and angry too. "That's not a name . . .?"

I tried to cock my head as if I couldn't see. He hit me across the face. Not hard, almost like from habit, but he still cut me.

"Tell me who you are. Tell me what is wrong with all these people." He hadn't heard of me, a lot of people hadn't then. Anyway they can't keep track of everybody. I wished I could have one of my tubes. I'd feel good then, I knew with a tube I could face anything.

"The suckling time is over. Why are they not sleeping? What they are doing does not exist. We don't recognise it. We do not recognise it. Bad . . . it is very *bad*." He moved away. His chair swivelled as he looked around the room again. I started to edge along the wall. The Teacher almost stood up. Shaking with rage he wheeled forward and started trying to boot the couples apart.

"Something has been done to my people, they are not like this really." The Boy was edging away too.

"You!" The Teacher whirled and spat in my face. The bandage took most of it, but I wear parts bare. Even though it was a Teacher's spit it was horrible. I started to get so that I couldn't stand it any more. Hell! I thought, what's it all for? How could you stand it? Why didn't we all just cut our throats?

"You and your illegal candyfloss!" I stood very still, trying not to cry with rage. I wondered where he'd heard of my floss. He lunged forward on his quick wheels.

"Lift your forelock!" I did that. He looked long and hard at my forehead. "FALSE SCAR!" he screamed suddenly, in my face.

That weapon was a foot from my chest. I saw his thumb move on the plate. I sat down. Suddenly, hard, all the way to the floor.

As I did that the Boy kicked the back of the Teacher's

14

chair and spun it like a top. The charge for his weapon sliced into the thin wall. Aluminium ran down like wax. Sparks shorted behind.

My backside stung like hell. Maybe it was the jerk, or maybe I meant to fire anyway, I don't think so, I don't think I meant to fire.

Both barrels of my other powder gun went off at once. The front of my tray burst out like a matchbox and the Teacher went over backwards. There was the smell of burned rubber from the aluminium splash on my sleeve. I don't think I meant to do it, I really don't.

The Teacher was trying to scream but he couldn't because most of his throat and chest was gone. He came forward on to his own lap as if he was trying to hide the blood and stuff there, as if he was ashamed of those human things. Then he must have stopped caring because he was dead.

I sat there wondering what in the world would I do. I mean, killing someone . . . I *mean* . . . killing a Teacher! It was the devil in me. I even thought maybe I should have had the evil taken out at the Rites. Teachers were so Lucky, so *sacred*!

"Come on!" The Boy got up off the floor. "He's dead . . . you can't change that!" He waited for me at the door. "Come on! He's *dead!*"

His great eyes stared at me out of the gloom. Right then he was frightened and that was what decided me. If he was scared I should be too. I was too numb to feel anything—but I sure understood that I had to go.

I got off the shattered tray and threw it on to a man on the floor. I left the gun in it, I'd be happier with two, but one was enough.

"God!" said the Boy. "You're treacherous!"

"Sure." They'd hang that man when they found him near my tray with the gun that killed a Teacher. I knew that, I had to survive and I didn't have to be just to do it. There was only one thing I was sure of and that was that I had to survive.

"Telling them all that. Whipping them up, then reporting them! You bastard!" He half admired it.

My head ached. God, but I needed a tube! If I could

only have my tube I knew I'd feel good again. I knew I'd done bad things . . . I felt tired and dirty. Killing that Teacher! I couldn't even think about that. Under it all I just knew I had to survive.

If I didn't preach, who'd lift the race out of our coming extinction as we dwindled and dwindled again? Who'd fight the Rites and the Teachers? The Saver? When the hell would he come? What was he *doing*? I wondered if Exploration Corps and the Saver was all a tale along with the Great Robot, just another Teacher's yarn to keep us quiet.

"The lies you tell! The foul things you do . . ." The Boy shook his head. "How can you do it? How can you stand to be you?"

I'd wondered that too. But really I knew what I was doing and why, I told myself it was important. Men like me, I had to survive . . . do what I did. I had to try and preach and change the world . . . I was exceptional and I had to do it.

"You don't have to believe it," I said. "You don't have to do what you're told. If you believe everything you're told, you deserve what people do to you. They deserved what they got back there." We went out into the street. Behind us a woman started to cry.

"Things are what you believe they are," said the Boy. I didn't want to think about that so I said nothing.

Then Wolf caught up with us. He's like that, he follows me everywhere, but he doesn't like the bangs.

CHAPTER TWO

BUT HELL! I hadn't meant to kill any Teacher! I never intended to kill anyone, it wasn't in me . . . not to *kill*. It wasn't possible, it couldn't happen. Unthinkable! It *hurt* . . . I didn't know which way, I was all upside down.

We were out on the pavement. I'd stopped, just thinking about it. I hadn't even decided which way to run.

"Come on!" The Boy pushed at me. Out in the Street the Whistler snapped shut. The rockets fired, it began to revolve slowly, then it flashed out of sight back down the Street.

The Teacher's chair swivelled and began to come out after us. The corpse jerked as it bounced over the threshold, some loose blood splashed on the floor.

That chair came like a dog. Radiating like hell, I had no doubt, telling just exactly where we were and what I'd done.

Pretty soon the body would start to smell—it was warm in the Streets—it'd be following us all the time . . . jerking those dead arms until they fell off, or until the other Teachers got me.

The Boy turned suddenly and pounced. The chair tried to get away but he held it and began to try and tip the body out. The lower part was easy enough but the head was attached by the leads. The Boy screwed up his face when he saw all that blood and damage.

I wasn't surprised. There were eighty-four of my bullets to the pound, I loaded each barrel with twenty of them and they each had a little wire tail an inch long. At range the tails kept them straight, and they only stung or bruised at distance anyway, but in close the tails thrashed about and that could really make a mess out of you. Teachers are as light as vanity anyway, like birds, no bones to speak of, but there was sure blood on that chair. I didn't remember using the guns on any man before, not in close to kill like that.

"Come on!" gasped the Boy. He was very pale and I thought he might vomit. I swam up out of my dream and went over to help his struggle with the chair. In the end we kicked the thing out over the edge of the pavement and into the airstream up the Street.

It sailed almost straight across, bounced off the far side and went down slowly. Cloth, rags and arms of Teacher streamed behind it, the body too, still attached by the head. We threw the legs part out. That went up, it was the lightest part.

"Come on!" said the Boy and we ran for it.

Two hundred yards up the Street we had to rest. Or the

Boy did, I just needed a tube. It was a hard climb up that spiral ramp around the Street, hard to walk, never mind run. What we had to do was get off the Street and into the girders of whatever there was behind.

"Yes," said the Boy. "Treacherous . . . you're that all right." He thought for a moment. "Do you have an excuse? Is this the way things are? What would you say makes you like that?"

I remembered to turn my head as if I was searching for his voice. I didn't speak. I thought about how I could get away and how soon I could have a tube. In the light I could see he was younger than I'd thought. Twelve, maybe, his skin creamy and smooth, his face very clean.

"Mind," he went on. "You can sing. You can certainly preach. You got them stirred all right, you certainly did! Interesting . . ." He giggled shrilly. "Those old women!" Then he went to the edge of the Street and looked down. "Time to go. Get up, old man, get stirred!" I don't feel so old . . . no, not at all, not really.

There was a manhole a foot above the pavement. The Boy prised it off with a knife he had. He guided me through and put my feet on the girder beyond. It was dark in there and through my bandage it was darker than ever.

The girders were to support the Streets, keep them apart and upright. Everything went through there, all the nutrient pipes to the Dispensers, everything. It was dank as well as dark. There were small lights, all uneven and wide spaced, a lot broken down. One was under a splashing, stinking amber waterfall . . . it had a halo of bright, flying drops and a small, incomplete rainbow too. At first there was a handrail, but soon it ended in a rusted, narrow spike.

The girders were twenty feet thick, three feet wide. We had to walk along and try to forget the vast darkness below. You couldn't hear any splash as that waterfall hit bottom—if there was such a thing. All the time there were noises from the Streets, the music beating in the reek of ammonia, the smell of rotting things.

You had to be careful where the girders were decayed. Some had been replaced and those were fairly good, but others had been patched up with slabs of welded concrete, all uneven and ready to trip you. I groped with my feet,

18

kept a tight hold on my dog. I wasn't pretending to be blind any more and I didn't like it.

We saw rats. Or heard them, the Dispenser pipes leaked and that fed them, they certainly weren't very active. Once I thought I heard voices and the Boy said he'd found people living in there, but that they didn't mean a thing. Sometimes there were plants growing near the lights, but they weren't worth much either.

Then we came to a white metal ladder leading up one of the verticals. It was perfect, in all the decay it was new. The Boy said we should change levels so we climbed up there. My foot, slimy from the girders, slipped and I nearly went. It was the Boy getting an arm around my shoulders that saved me. He steadied me in the dripping water and I grunted while I got my feet back on. His arm and chest felt soft and I hated it even through my rubbers. I hoped I wouldn't end owing him too much, I hoped I wasn't getting to like him.

We edged on round the great Street cylinders as they rose sheer through the girder forest. Some of them sagged, there was a whole area like that, lights showed through where the structure had sunk and pulled apart and it lit the place a little. There were thousands of Streets, mostly they weren't more than a few feet apart.

I don't remember it too well. It just seemed like an age. Holding the Boy's soft hand, edging along those dangerous girders, wishing I could let go whatever I was clinging to long enough to give myself a tube. I was never so cold . . . the girders groaned and moved, it was filthy in there. I was lucky in my rubbers but the Boy got lagged.

Then I looked through a chink in one of the Streets and it was too far down. There were no buildings in that one, just the ramp, with a handrail and lights that went away until they converged. You couldn't see any end, only a mist down there and the lights vanishing into a haze of gold. The wind ruffled my hair, I took my head out and saw the Boy looking at me.

"Fresh air?" I made it sound like a question. I don't know how long I fooled him that I was blind.

"This is where we get out," he said. I was glad to hear it.

He unlocked a manhole and we crawled on to the empty

pavement. Someone had been there. There were some rat bones by a charred place and someone had scratched something short and obscene about Teachers on the wall. The Boy closed the manhole and we started up the ramp.

We were near the surface. It took twenty minutes and we were out. It was dark, the wind whined around the gantry. We went up the slope into the night and no one saw us go.

We stopped in the lichen woods at the top. I lay down but I couldn't sleep, there were bad things on my mind. I wanted a tube but I didn't take one. Sometimes I liked to see how long I could go without; but I just got sad and everything seemed dark. Anyway, I couldn't take one with the Boy there, it was a thing I had to hide . . . I didn't know why.

I kept seeing that Teacher's legs flailing up there against the sky. I almost wished I'd gone down, got hid in the dark or light—which ever it was—down at the Street bottoms. Given myself up and gone to the Rites maybe, got my brains burned and everything finished with. They'd never tell me my name now I'd killed a Teacher . . . I didn't see what I had to hope for.

Dawn came and I stood up. The Boy got up too, he hadn't spent much of a night. I'd heard him thrashing and turning, there were black bags under his eyes. He was wet and cold from the dripping trees, he kept rolling close to me in the night, for the warmth, I thought. I'd just eased away, he sure looked angry that morning.

"Come on!" he said. We went through the woods, not saying anything, I walked behind, thinking about that Teacher. I wouldn't have gone if he hadn't ordered me.

I kept wondering *why*, what Purpose could I have? What evil had that Teacher done? Sure, he'd split my lip, but he was entitled, I couldn't blame him for that. I was just old, blind Candy Man, they did what they liked to people and everyone thought they were sacred.

But there was a contradiction. Teachers were only agents really, agents of the Machine that lived deep down and ran things. We loved them . . . *the Teachers* . . . what they meant . . . it was funny, me loving Teachers and hating what was behind them and what they did.

I suppose you liked them because people always told you how good they were right from when you could listen. But. . . when you started *thinking* . . . they were in the way really, the Teachers and their rules. They were good, or they made you believe they were good, but if you had a brain left that wasn't burned, then sooner or later you'd got to stomp them because they were in your way. Stomp them and feel bad about it.

The sun came up and I felt better. We came to a place overlooking a Street and I sat down out of the wind to warm up.

"You coming or not?" The Boy still looked wet and angry. I said nothing. I stayed where I was. I wasn't too bad, I had my rubbers.

'Gas-tight suit quantity one,' it said on the box when I found it. Rubber, or some sort of plastic stuff, it was made with hooks and loops all over it. Orange, it had been orange once, but with age and dirt it'd gone to a dingy flesh colour. It was skin tight all over, quite thin, a waterproof zip started under the crotch and ran to my neck. I'd found them in some ruins and they were pretty important to me, they kept me from having to touch the world, the world from touching me. I hated mirrors too, my eye bandage stopped me from seeing too much of things . . .

Right then I was cold, but I wasn't wet like the Boy and the night rain and wet leaves had cleaned off most of the dirty water from the girders. The Boy still stank of it, perhaps that why he was so angry.

"You coming?" He stood there. I grinned. It was hard to keep staring straight ahead as if I was blind. "They'll come soon. They'll get you!" He walked slowly away. "You won't have a chance!" He stopped a few yards off. "I think you ought to be more careful . . ." Then he got really shrill and angry. "You're not coming? All right then!" He went off along the edge of the trees, struck diagonally down across the hillside to get across the valley and past the Street.

I broke the seal and let the first tube roll out on to my palm. I threw the motto away—I never read them, they were just crazy meaningless symbols. I broke the end off

21

the tube and squeezed a drop out. It looked like a good one; when I'd split the rubbers of my arm I plugged it in and lay back to let it work.

Sunlight came warming through the trees. The lichens turned from grey to marbled green, to all the pastel harmonies of beauty. Small white flowers showed on the trees, the few leaves brightened, the trunks were dark in greens and blues. It was really beautiful. I relaxed.

Seventeen lovely aircraft rode south on the sound of a thousand choirs . . . bright striped napalm tanks like jewels under the silver beauty of their swallow's wings. The dog lay lolling his coral tongue at me.

I sat up. Man . . . but I had to get away! The Boy had gone. Out of sight . . . maybe it had been that long. I wondered why he'd helped me, poor old Candy Man . . . he hadn't liked me, but he'd seemed to care. I wondered why he should be interested. I threw away the empty tube and wondered how long it'd been. He couldn't have walked so far.

I stood up to see better. There was the end of a Street a thousand feet below me. It was the same one. Where I'd killed the Teacher. I wondered how I'd got back that way. Then I slipped back again and started admiring the beauty of it down there.

The rubbish ring was all star brilliant in the clarity of the tube. As I watched something yellow came up in the air stream, turned in the air, scattered, came down like coloured snow. There was beauty in its path, a logic in its fall. I smiled and looked, something was streaming yellow and brilliant from the gantry.

Then there was a Whistler. It locked on the gantry and opened. I nodded to myself, that was beautiful too. Teachers wheeled out and machines too. For a while they rolled about down there, the wheels cutting arabesque patterns in the soft ground. Clear, lovely, rhythmic designs. Like writing. I tried to read them for the great wisdom there, and all the time I knew they'd kill me if they caught me and that I ought to be running.

They found something and they all converged . . . focused on it, a focal point, a node in the grand design. I screwed my eyes, looked really hard and it was the

Teacher's legs they'd found. Lying there, slack twisted, like a strand of broken string. They gathered them up, put them in some sort of white basket and took it back to the Whistler. I was almost crying. The blood, all that blood had dried black.

Then they turned to their machines. It dawned on me again that it was time to go. Before they picked up my body heat, my smell or my vibrations or something. Suddenly I was as worried as I'd been happy.

I turned and jogged into the woods. There were stones in my pathway, there were thorns too, thorns and clutching branches. My rubbers saved me and I didn't have to touch the lichen either. Later there was small tight gorse about knee high and it was like running through treacle. When I looked down the tiny spikes had cleaned my suit, taken the old dirt off as high as my knees. After a while there was a high buzzing—but I thought that was the tube—I thought that was just in my head.

CHAPTER THREE

I WENT ON crashing through the intricate angle that was the lichen woods. All the time there was that beautiful humming and the wind soughed soft songs through the branches. Altogether I don't remember much except that I was happy and there were fearful things behind coming to get me and I was laughing a lot as I ran.

Then I was running downhill. Suddenly I came blundering out into the open.

I ducked back into the trees and lay panting. A millipede crawled on my arm and I smiled at it. Aeroplanes went over low going north. There was what looked like a sunset with black smoke to the south. My tube was fading and my rubbers were torn. I could see flesh and I was suddenly too worried to care.

I got my gun and checked the loads. All the time I cursed myself for being careless. Anything could have happened. I wouldn't go so long without a tube again, it hit too much when you broke the fast. The pyrites was gone from the wheels and the barrels were full of sewage from the girders. I sat up to clean it out. When I'd finished that buzzing was still there, it'd never stopped.

It wasn't the tube any more, I was over that. I turned quickly and the Boy was hovering a few feet above and just behind me. He was just under the tree tops, he grinned at me.

"Come down?" he said.

"OK." I slipped the gun to where I could get it quick. He drifted down and landed beside me. The buzzing stopped.

That Boy could fly! It didn't surprise me. I'd been around too long, nothing surprised me any more. But it made him something special. It took me a moment to understand that he was flying, tubes left me like that sometimes after a long fast. Left me stupid, I mean.

I suppose it was my expression while I figured out if was a dream or not that kidded him I was blind. I guess my stupid face fooled him even though I stared straight at him. People think you're stupid if you're blind.

"Hullo," he said. He smiled a great big smile at me. I noticed how sharp and white his teeth were. He seemed to have forgotten how angry he'd been, I didn't speak, I looked a bit to his left and frowned.

"You're *blind*," he said. It might almost have been a question. "You're no good. But she said . . ." Then he smiled again, but coldly, like not with his eyes. "Maybe you're interesting . . . but you should hurry. There's a pack of Teachers coming through the woods!"

He paused. He licked his lips. He talked as if he was trying to fool me we hadn't met before. It was daft, I'd have known his voice even if I was blind. He was making it sound deeper . . . rougher, but I'd still have known.

"It *is* you they want—isn't it?" He licked his lips again. "You know what they'll do if they catch you?" I didn't say anything. "They'll break you on their wheels. They'll tear out your heart. They'll take your kidneys . . . they'll *vivisect* you!"

He was watching me closely, all the time he was looking

24

for some sign of fear. I watched him run his hand up the silky hair of his arm. He wasn't as boyish as all that . . . there was a fuzz of blond beard that you could see shine in the sun.

When I still didn't say anything, when I didn't roll about in fear or beg to be saved he looked disappointed and started to call me names. A baboon, a blind fool, some kind of monkey too.

"Maybe you're not . . ." He started moving sideways to get behind me. "I'LL FIX YOU! I'll break your back and leave you for them! I'll laugh when they take you away!" I whirled and he was shaping to kick me.

"Useless blind man!" I brought up my gun. He had great heavy metal soles on his shoes, he looked a lot tougher than before.

He saw the gun coming. He yelped. Twisted his body out of the line, he held his arms above his head like a dancer. He buzzed and started to soar up. Even at that moment, I swear, he was enjoying the grace of the movement. I fired.

I knew I hadn't put bullets in the gun when I cleaned it. There was just the powder and the packing. I only meant to sting him, to frighten him off.

The blast took him across the lower belly and he somersaulted, crashed back against a tree there. He screamed as he went and the impact knocked him cold.

I stood and listened. I could hear the Teachers now. Their machines were cutting right through the trees, they were only half a mile away.

The buzzing started again and the Boy started to go up. He was still out. I saw his clothes torn away and still burning across his stomach. There weren't any guts hanging out, but his genitals had a sooty, burned look about them. He'd just been unlucky and stopped the wadding.

He wore a sort of belt under his clothes. A slim thing, decorated, flat white metal boxes every two inches around it. It was what lifted him. He went up very slowly, his body folded at forty-five degrees, his arms hanging straight down. Then he lodged in the tree and floated against the lower branches, still out cold. The Teachers were getting nearer, I could hear them.

I jumped, got the Boy's ankle and dragged him down. I snapped the belt off him and pushed it through the loops on my rubbers. If a boy could use it I didn't see why I couldn't. It took to the last fastener and then it was tight. I found a small lead that ended in a sucker just behind his ear so I took it and put it behind my own. His flesh was sure soft. I tried not to touch him, but I felt it once through my gloves. It wasn't only the world I hated to touch, I didn't like to touch people either, unless they ordered me I wouldn't.

The underbrush crackled. They weren't a hundred yards away. I dragged some dead leaves over the Boy. Hell, it was the least I could do, he saved me in the Street and later in the girders. We'd been through things together. I wondered why he'd saved me then and tried to give me to the Teachers now . . . but I hoped they'd find him. It'd give me a little time while they questioned him, executed him for his part. When I looked back I saw a foot left uncovered, sticking out of the leaves.

The first machines came through the trees. Great blades threw up gouts of wood and leaves. Lichen clumps came shaking down.

"Away!" I screamed in my mind. "GET AWAY!"

The belt picked me up by the middle and I belched. I got Wolf by the handle as I passed. It didn't take me very high. We raced down the hill, six inches up, accelerating all the way.

My rubbers spread the loads over my body but the belt still pulled hell out of me. It seemed to know where it was going so I didn't interfere. It was away from the Teachers and that was enough. Anyway, I was being sick, so I just let it take me on.

The Teachers fired. There were hot air blasts and ozone smell as the charges cracked past. I can still see the ground wrench as the belt zig-zagged between the shots. I can still feel my face tugging out of shape in the changing directions. Those belts took a bit of riding until you got the trick.

Behind the hill was glowing under black smoke and the air was red and green and violet. Ionization they call that, you saw it when the Teachers fired a lot.

Most of the shooting was now at low power, but someone was using full charges. I saw no more, right then the belt whisked me over the first hill range.

We passed dozens of Streets, the belt dodged them all, carried me close under the tree lines, where there were never any people.

I saw a couple of settlements too, in places where the Streets were sparse. Farmers there watched me go, their jaws hanging. I almost felt good then. Once I waved, but no one waved back. I was surprised to see so many people on the surface, it's remarkable what people can do away from Teachers and off the Streets.

The belt started to slow, I wished I'd had time to load my gun. We came down over some high trees, my feet swished through leaves and we dropped into this big clearing around a low house with a big chimney out at the back.

I didn't want to go up to the house. Not yet anyway. The belt obediently dropped me amongst tree stumps and brambles fifty yards from the building. It had to be where the Boy had come from. I'd hurt him. I had his belt. If there was anyone else they might not like that.

The belt stopped buzzing so I took it off and put it in the pouch on the back of my rubbers. Then I sat down and loaded my gun. I started to feel better then.

I crawled up behind some nettles and began to watch the house. That chimney wasn't a part of it. I could see how far back it was now, up the slope, set at a distance. There was honeysuckle growing on the house. The window frames were white, but there seemed to be no glass in them. The walls had been whitewashed once, but that was mostly gone and I could see they were built of slate. The door was about a foot open. There was nothing moving.

It was pleasant lying in the sun. I even thought I might lay my rubbers open. I did take them off sometimes, when there was clean water I always washed. There were insects humming and some butterflies. Once in a while there'd be a warm puff of breeze that would ruffle the grass and bring the scent of roses. The place seemed to radiate peace. It was so hot the oils began to come out of the stock of my gun.

After a long time there was still nothing happening so I

got up carefully, moved from stump to stump towards the Cottage. I got closer and closer and I didn't make a sound all the way.

The window wood was weathered white and not painted like I'd thought. There was glass in the windows too, but it didn't shine and you couldn't see through it. It all looked as if no one had been there for years. On the left, up the hill, in a gully, there was a crashed aeroplane. All bulged alloy and flaked green paint. One of the engines was broken loose, you could see twisted turbine blades. A broken ejector seat was half buried farther up the hill, just below a three legged Speaker . . . I could see a thin, white gleam of bones up there, it'd all been like that for years.

There was some blackened grease on the door hinges, but they were heavy with rust as well. I held my weapon ready with one hand and pushed with the other.

I got a splinter and the door opened smoothly and evenly, without a sound. When it was fully open there was a click and it stayed there as if it'd never moved. It was perfect. The rust didn't even crumble. I was so surprised I stepped in without thinking.

There was a movement over there across the room in the dusty gold half light. I pointed my gun over there and it was a man. He looked at me once and then went on with what he was doing.

I moved out of the light of the door and into the shadows to the left. My head bumped a beam and some dust came down on my shoulders.

It was warm in there. A fly droned. Nothing happened. I kept watching the man. When nothing had happened for five minutes I went across to see what he was doing, to see what was so important to him.

It was pottery. He was decorating pottery. He had brushes he'd made by stuffing hair inside quills and tying it there with a small tight whip of thread. Once in a while he'd reach to dip the brush in something he had ground up on a small slab. Sometimes he'd turn the pot and then go on painting on the new surface. When he finished a pot he'd put it on a tray to his left and reach another from the right. He didn't stop and he didn't look at me. Once he wiped his hands, but he went right on working.

I stood there at his elbow for five minutes feeling foolish and then a cat with dark ears and a light brown face came in at the window. It saw me and stared a long time. For a moment its eyes were crossed, then they looked straight at me, then they were crossed again. It twitched its tail and went away.

The Potter went on working, timbers creaked as the roof moved with the heat. That's the difference between the high and low ground, hot and cold, summer and winter.

"All right!" said a voice outside. It wasn't the Boy. "I'll see to it!" A man came through the door. I turned quickly to face him.

He filled the door. He was seven feet tall and he was so heavy he still looked fat. He wore a suit like mine, but it was new and clean, unfastened down the front. He had a long whip thing with a reel of thread at one end, there was a light patch of armour on his right shoulder. On the armour the cat crouched looking at me as if I was a bird. Its tail twitched. It was a very big cat, with long claws, I suppose that was why he needed the armour.

The Fat Man put the whip and the fish he had with it on to the table. He walked across towards me. He ignored my gun and smiled. He held up his left hand to show it was empty, he used his right to steady the cat.

I stood still. I wasn't supposed to be able to see anything.

"Ah . . . over here. No—don't point the gun at me, I don't like that." He looked strong, fine, he wasn't flabby fat. Clean and confident. I knew my shot would bounce off him, or he'd turn them away with his gaze or something. I wished I was like him, I wished I was him.

"Tell me . . ." He was looking at my gun. "Is it ancient? Is it an old one, or did you make it yourself?"

"Don't believe it," said the cat. "Don't believe it whatever he says. He can see. Saw me. Watching the Potter too." My dog stiffened and suddenly growled.

I watched. I almost hoped it'd speak again. I thought perhaps then I could be sure if I believed it. Funny things happened in my brain sometimes.

"I'm just poor blind Candy Man . . ."

"Stop lying!" It did it again, the cat was talking all right.

Now I looked I could see it wasn't just a cat. It was a big animal in good condition, there was something that wasn't a bell around its neck and there was a connection from it up to behind its ear, like the one on the flying belt. The animal hung on the man's shoulder as if it had taken root. I lowered my gun. I mean, I didn't know what they could do to me. The Potter kept on working, over his shoulder I could see a waterwheel slowly turning.

"So you're Candy Man," the Fat Man stood with his hands on his hips. "So you're the blind man K's been telling us about. So you made it here. Where's K?"

"I'm just poor Candy . . . I don't mean any harm." It was true. I never mean any harm . . .

"Except to Teachers." Maybe they hadn't heard what I'd done to the Boy, I guessed that he must be K.

"I didn't mean it. Accident . . ."

"And you're blind?" The question was like a knife.

"Yes—"

"No!" said the cat. "He's not! He's a liar. He's treacherous . . ."

"Why the gun? How do you use that?"

"By sound . . . I know . . . I *know* where things are."

"He'll kill us all! He'll betray us!"

"K wants him. K said he might be blind. K thinks he's interesting. K's convinced!"

That was good enough for me. If it was good enough for the Boy it ought to do for them.

"K can be wrong, we know what K's like." That cat was still glaring at me with its velvet eyes. "He's dangerous."

"K wants him. K thinks at least he'll be worth study. Get us some good answers. The effects of his life. Basically he's human. Just think of that!"

"I am. Dangerous. K's too interested in evil things. A sickness."

"Humanity. It's K's study. Would you tell K it was sick?"

The cat went silent then. It seemed to shrug its shoulders. All that while they'd forgotten me. I had time to wonder what was going on. Sure there were some funny people about, but this was different. I mean, although I'd seen stranger things I'd never seen a talking cat before, or I didn't remember any. These people, they could *fly*, they were clean too. And it was as if they had *powers*. Confidence. They were different, there was something attractive about them. I thought of the Saver, but I dismissed that. I didn't even allow that possibility to myself.

"We'll wait for K," said the Fat Man and that seemed to finish the discussion. It looked like I had to wait for K too. From what they spoke of him he was important. I hoped his belly wasn't hurting too much.

The Fat Man went to the back of the room and pushed at something. The wall moved back like a curtain.

There were dials and small screens in a narrow band right across the wall. The man passed something silver in his hand over something there and the strip came alive in flashing light patterns and that same humming as the belts made.

The Fat Man glanced here and there, tapped something and then spoke. Mostly it was numbers in relationships I didn't understand, then he stopped talking and listened for a while. Once the cat leaned forward and said something too. I didn't understand that either.

I got up as if to stretch my legs. They were still talking and listening and I walked right past them. On the left there was something I hadn't seen before.

White metal. White, flexible metal, hanging in folds behind one of the other doors. Bulky, as if they were meant to wear over everything. There were domed clear helmets to go with them, there were straps and loops all over and tubes with valves led down the legs. There were scientific looking things strapped all over the shoulders, there were big orange letters painted on the front. I knew what they were. They were Corps suits. The regalia you got if you passed the Rites and got into Exploration Corps. They were that or something very like it.

I walked on past as if nothing had happened. I even groped round a chair but that was wasted because they were still busy with the flickering wall. I made it into the sunlight.

Fifty yards out in the brambles I turned and the cat was sitting on the doorstep watching me. I sat on a stump and got out a tube. I saw the cat's dark tail flick as I slotted it in. We watched each other. With that super vision I get soon after a tube I started to count the cat's fur. I got to nine hundred thousand and sixty, they were taking on rainbow colours, and the cat got up as if it had been called and went into the Cottage, the magenta tail with the nine thousand and sixty hairs waving high.

I got up quickly and went up the quietly pulsing hill to where the Speaker Box stood on its elegant legs beneath the indigo and cerulean sky.

There was beautiful music near the Speaker. I saw that Teacher's face when I shot him. I closed my eyes and shuddered as I saw the legs go windmilling up the Street.

But I didn't care about any of that. I had them. I had that Corps party cold where I wanted them. They were breaking the rules. Either you pass the Rites and you're on the Corps side, or your place is in the Streets and they've burned out your brain for you. Of course there was me, but there weren't many of us—freedom always was the hard way. As I got still nearer I picked out the Dispenser, a little pool of nutrient by it and a fat, sleeping squirrel.

Maybe K, that admirable Fat Man, even the cat, maybe they were trying to do good. I recognised the possibility. Maybe they were the beginning of the Saver even, I allowed that too, but I didn't believe it, or maybe I didn't care. I knew I'd do what I decided in the house. I'd do that and please the Teachers. I thought perhaps it'd make up for killing one of them. There was the Boy too. I didn't want to wait for him to come back, there was too much risk in that. Anyway, this time I'd decided to ask for my name again.

I opened the box and looked in at the Speaker. After a moment the machine answered.

"Name?"

"A report . . ."

"These lenses . . . your voice isn't clear."

There was an old helmet over the lens, I lifted it off. There was mud in the Speaker. I screwed it out with my

32

finger and the music got louder. Who'd do a thing like that? Fancy soiling a Teachers' Speaker!

"Now then?"

"Corps men here. Living in our country. Spreading discontent, abusing women. Sodomy . . . rape . . ." I didn't know that, but you had to make it sound good, I didn't expect to understand what they'd really come for, I mean, they were the *Corps.*

"Thank you."

"Not all. A man here. Making pottery, he's got a *waterwheel*! I think that's what it is." Technology isn't allowed either.

"So." There was a moment's silence. Maybe the machine was shocked.

"Not all. They call me Candy Man . . . I want a name . . . you said you'd give me a name . . . ?"

The tubes clicked out of the reward slot. I gathered the pack into my palm. I opened my mouth again to ask about my name and that cat hit me in the back of the neck with all four paws. I sprawled forward into the brambles. I heard my dog growling and the Fat Man shouting behind me.

CHAPTER FOUR

MY TUBES WENT flying. I felt claws slice up my cheeks. I tried to get up. That cat weighed over twenty pounds. I was wondering what it would be like to die of a cat when the Fat Man came up.

Don't think I was doing nothing. I had the cat round the middle and I could feel it pulsing inside. I thought how I'd soon stop that and it opened up the backs of my hands for me. I saw the claws were made of stainless steel.

I threw it off as far as I could. Almost five yards. It came back for me walking sideways and showing its small, deadly teeth. My dog was making growling noises and making short rushes at it as it came, but he had more

33

sense than actually to take it on. The cat ignored him and kept on coming.

"*Denied*," came the steady voice of the Speaker. "*No name.*"

"So that's it! You do these things for that?" The Fat Man waved his hand at the cat and it sat down and started licking itself. Cats have some pretty dirty habits, I thought how I'd settle with that creature, strangle it when the Teachers came . . . in the confusion then.

"It fits," said the Fat Man. "Maybe K . . ."

"He's treacherous," said the cat. Then it told the Fat Man what I'd done.

"Fool," said the man. "They want *you*, remember? What do you think they'll do to you? Let you off for turning us in?"

At that moment I'd forgotten that. I'd really forgotten killing that Teacher, maybe it was that I didn't want to remember. I'd forgotten it like it'd never happened . . . that was what I wanted, that it'd never happened. Then again I wanted my name, that was urgent . . . serious, that and getting regular tubes.

"See," said the cat. "He's just like the others. All he wants is to please the Teachers!"

"You can't blame him. He's got to want his name. It's his condition. They got him young, made him . . . re-made him. If they rang bells he'd salivate!"

"Stupid dog!" Maybe you haven't heard a cat laugh. It's a mad sort of sound. The tubes were lying at my feet so I picked them up.

"You can do without that." The Fat Man sounded almost kind. Maybe it was a trap. I didn't know. "We can fix you something better. You don't have to depend on Teachers."

I thought about that. I wasn't so sure that I wanted to be without the tubes, even if it was possible. They were all there was for me really. Until I had my name and Purpose they made the world possible, without them I knew I'd just stop.

"We ought to go." The cat sat up straight. It pricked its ears and turned its head through a hundred and eighty degrees to look behind it. "No time for him. No time for social work. Never mind what K says . . . we've got to go!'"

"Just get lost," said the man to me. "Remember the Teachers are coming and it's you they want." He thought for a moment. "If it turns out K still wants you we can always find you . . ."

They turned and walked quickly towards the house. After a few steps the cat began to run, leaping and bobbing, tail vertical through the long grass. My dog barked a couple of times, but that was just to show he was still on my side.

I didn't need telling I had to go. The woods were close, but there was a deep gully so it took me a few minutes to reach the blue-green safety. At the first trees I looked back and saw the man and the cat disappear through the cottage door. I watched it shut behind them.

I had time to think how easily they'd let me off and then the aeroplanes came. They were fifty feet up but it looked lower. They were so fast you hardly saw them. The shock wave knocked me down.

Then I saw the planes again as they pulled up two miles beyond the clearing, hurtling up and away on the black plumes of their afterburners.

Then the first explosion happened right next to the house. The whole clearing burst into a sea of flame in that same instant. I couldn't see what happened. I could hardly face the heat, but I saw the other explosions in the fire and the burning things go twisting up.

My rubbers started to stink so I ran into the trees. There was just the roar of fires and the distant murmur of jet engines. I reckoned everybody must have been killed. I didn't see how any man could have survived in the particular reds and yellows of that inferno. A breeze began to disturb the leaves. I wondered what to do next, then turned and walked slowly away. I didn't risk the buzz of the fly-belt with the Teachers about.

Half a mile on I met the Boy. He was walking and running, making what time he could towards the smoke behind me.

"What happened?" was what he said. I told him some planes had hit the house in the clearing back there. That there'd been a waterwheel there and maybe that was why, that, anyway, the Teachers' planes hit anywhere they felt like. Hell, they hit places every day, you couldn't expect to know the logic of it.

"See anyone?" He seemed to have forgotten the last time we'd met. I couldn't see where I'd shot him, he didn't seem to be in any pain. I didn't remind him.

"I heard a potter guy," I said. "I heard him and a big man calling a cat . . ." The Boy cocked his head and smiled, then picked at his mouth with the silver thing I first thought was a toothpick.

"So you spoke to the Teachers?" He wasn't armed. He didn't seem angry, but I kept my gun ready all the time. "Oh, never mind. I know you can't help it, I understand you must have your name, be told your purpose. I want to work on you. You come with me, they'll be OK if they made the cottage."

"What about the Teachers?"

"Maybe they won't come after the planes. Anyway, I can deal with any Teachers." I knew he could. He was something special. There was a delicacy about him to look at . . . those slender hands, he was just a kid. Still young to go to the Rites . . . but he'd looked tougher on the hill and he'd survived the fight there. He was something special. I decided that maybe I'd find out about him, what made him so. Perhaps it'd be worth my name. I nodded, I'd go back with him. Anyway, it'd been an order.

He didn't seem in any hurry. I kept listening for Teachers. As we got towards the clearing there was smoke and the tree tops had been ripped to shreds. I made myself walk steady beside him, all the time I was worrying about the Teachers.

We reached the clearing just exactly when they did. The Whistler came in over the trees on the one side as we came to the other.

We dropped on our stomachs and watched the thing looking for a landing place in that churned clearing.

Here and there stumps were burning still, columns of smoke went up in the wavering air. You could see raw black earth scars where the explosions had ripped the ground. Rusting things, old machinery and weapons, were

36

revealed all lightly covered with white ash that had powdered down.

The house was still standing. There was only part of the roof hit, the regular pattern of the slates was hardly disturbed, the window frames looked charred and the door frame was still burning sluggishly. They'd only used high explosives, that and the fire jelly. If they'd used anything else we wouldn't have been standing there.

The Whistler settled in a cloud of ash. It opened the way they did and the Teachers came wheeling out. Some had those big broad wheels they used off the Streets. Groups of them hooked up like millipedes and then they could go over anything. They went all ways, fanning out, some of them were even walking.

They poked about in the clearing for a while, they seemed very interested in the plane wreck. Maybe, after the fire, it looked like one of the ones that did the bombing, the design hadn't changed for thousands of years. Why should it? Nothing else had. Some Teachers were up there busy repairing the Speaker on a new tripod. I didn't think anyone would deliberately destroy Teachers' property, but who could be choosy from a plane at a thousand miles an hour? The music hadn't stopped. It took more than bombs and a splash of fire to stop the music.

The Teachers moved out into a circle around the Cottage. One raised a hand and they started to move in.

"We can't have that," said the Boy, half to himself. Then, turning to me: "Come on!" He crouched up. "Stay close!" He moved into the clearing and I went after him.

It was dangerous, sure, but I knew the Boy was Lucky, that he was important to me, that he was *important*. Anyway, it was an order, I couldn't ignore what he said. Even then I suspected what he might do to those Teachers.

He held the Toothpick up to his mouth and I was close enough to hear him speak to it. Before I knew what was happening there was a puff of smoke from each of the Teachers and their arms jerked and they all sat still. It wasn't the Boy that did it, it was the Cottage. I saw the hatches close all along the lowest line of slates.

"Dead?"

37

The Boy nodded. I mean, a dozen Teachers, just like that! He saw my face and put the toothpick away.

"Killing . . ." He looked away for a moment, then back to me again. "I suppose . . . I suppose it's bad. I *know* it is, but I had to keep them out of the Cottage. I couldn't argue with Teachers, you can't reason with them." I thought how I could make a really good call in a minute, maybe a name's worth. "Anyway, they were really after you."

Then I thought how perhaps I wouldn't make that call. Maybe I did owe the boy something. You don't burn up a man's stomach and not owe him something, and in a way he'd just saved me again. Also he was my connection with the Fat Man and the Corps people, maybe I could find my way into the Corps through them.

We got across the gully and when we'd climbed up the other side the heat hit us like a wall. The ground was hot, I could feel it right through my boot soles and my rubbers began to feel soft. I knew I'd be OK—Wolf too—but I wasn't so sure about the Boy. After a minute he started using his fly-belt so he didn't feel a thing . . . he was Lucky to have another of those. There were all sorts of small burned animals and birds in the ash.

"Walk quickly," said the Boy. "I don't like flying, this belt hurts my tummy . . ." I looked at him quickly, but he was smiling to himself and he wasn't in any agony . . . like he'd been burned there, I mean. I don't know, I thought that maybe he really was sympathetic. He seemed to care about things, people, me. About how I might be suffering in that heat. I thought how he must have been angry with me up on the hill, before the Teachers came. I thought it might have been for slaughtering that Teacher in the Street, but then I thought of the dozen he'd just killed and I couldn't understand it. I just didn't *understand*.

Near the Cottage the heat was terrible. Some old metal things were red hot there. I slipped in a tube but for once I didn't feel any better. I still had to force myself on, maybe it took some of the pain away, perhaps that was all they did, that and letting me go on.

The chimney was down in a tumble of bricks. All up the slope the top was blown off the kiln, a woodpile was spread around it and still burning. Right in close to the Cottage you could see a cluster of craters, vivid blue on the ash, the clay scattered up the hill in long irregular splashes. As you looked you could see some of them slowly filling with steaming nutrient from a broken main.

The Boy pushed open the Cottage door with his foot and we went inside. The wall which covered the instruments was all twisted and blown out in bulges. In one place where it was burst you could see burn marks on the instruments behind. It was curious to see wood bent like that, but as I said, nothing surprises after I've had a tube. Maybe they were making them stronger, or putting new things in them, but I think it was just because I'd been fasting. It was as if anything could happen. There weren't any rules so why should I be surprised?

When I looked around the rest of the house it was amazing just how intact everything was. There were bomb fragments mashed into the table and floor where the roof was twisted. I counted them and calculated their forces and trajectories. Some hadn't come from the roof, a lot had come from the wall. A load of dust had come down but there wasn't any other damage. The pots weren't broken and that fish the Fat Man had brought in all that time ago was still wet. I realised how cool it was in there.

"Cool?" I said.

"Yes—protected." The Boy was over at the curtain wall just looking at it. "No good, can't use this. They've blown it."

"What? What can't we use?"

"We could escape here. That man you heard, that man and the cat. They blew it—left me behind. We'll have to go down. There may be Teachers again soon. I can't kill any more . . ."

He opened a locker hidden under one of the benches along the wall and took some gear out. One of the things was an interesting looking pistol that he stuck in his belt.

"Didn't even leave me a suit . . ." he said. "You can't be too careful. They must know who we are, maybe what we're after." He moved the pistol so it didn't dig into him too much.

"What *are* you after?" I asked, but he wouldn't answer.

He opened another smaller locker and waved his toothpick there. "I'll hide it better than them!"

He led us out into the heat and clear of the house. Then he looked back and spoke to his toothpick again. The house glowed blue for a moment, then bubbled and began to burn. Everything, the slates, the stones, everything burned away in small white flames. There wasn't any smoke.

"Come on!" said the Boy. "They used it to get away, that's why they couldn't destruct!" He led up the hill past the kiln. By the time we got past there none of the house was left. In all those ashes it might never have been there at all. Like I said, I'd stopped being surprised.

The kiln was a ten foot brick-lined slot up the hill. It was thirty feet from top to bottom. At the top it had collapsed and was mostly filled with bricks from the chimney. At the bottom there was an arched place where the fire would have been. The bricks were scattered with broken pottery and there was burning wood everywhere. It started to rain and then there was steam as well as smoke, drifting white mists moved across the clearing.

"This is the place." The Boy knelt at the bottom of the kiln. There were bricks there too, worn almost shapeless by the fire. He got one out with the point of a knife and the rest came more easily. There was a sheet of something shiny revealed then. There weren't any seams or joints in it but the Boy showed the middle part his toothpick and it swung open without being touched. There were steps down there and it was almost dark.

I looked back at the leaden sky. The Boy saw me look and asked how I expected the weather to stay good when the control was gone and told me to follow him.

It wasn't much of a staircase. Just a few turns of left spiral and we came to a dead end.

"Hold tight!" The Boy grabbed a handle there with one hand and waved the toothpick with the other. The floor dropped away and we went down like a lead weight.

It was only three minutes but it seemed like hours. There was no way of knowing if the thing would stop or even if there was any way of stopping it. It slowed very quickly and sent me sprawling on the floor. The Boy was

40

OK, he knew what was going to happen and he was holding on.

You couldn't see anything, it was a dark place. The white metal box we were in had a sort of glow about it, but two paces outside you couldn't see a thing.

"Black . . ." said the Boy. "You first, you're the blind man, you're used to it."

It was the girders again. Thicker maybe, vastly heavy, maybe four feet wide. I groped on with my feet, my hand locked on to Wolf's handle.

It was murder. Water and stuff kept falling on us again. I thought I could hear voices, mostly like they were weeping. You could only tell that they were far away below and that they weren't happy. I inched on trying to remember the exact direction, the number of steps between each upright, and when you got there you still had to find your way around them.

In fact it wasn't all that far. Suddenly Wolf snorted and something brushed across my feet. A light rectangle came on ahead and after a moment I saw it was a corridor leading away.

"You can thank God they left that for us!" said the Boy. "It's OK now Candy! There are lights!" I let him pass me and he went briskly up the corridor.

Twenty yards on there was a short spiral stair and when we'd climbed that we were at a dead end again. The Boy waved his magic toothpick and the wall above us hinged out of the way. We climbed through and we were in the dusty sunlight of another kiln, all roofed over, just like the other one before they'd bombed it. It wasn't reasonable, I didn't like it. It didn't seem right, standing there amongst the stacked pottery that I'd seen broken a few minutes before.

CHAPTER FIVE

IT WAS SO strange, being transported back like that. I'd been so sure we'd been going down all the way, through

41

all those great girders, there'd only been that short spiral up again. It'd turned me upside down, I didn't know which way to turn.

"You wait here," the Boy told me. "I've got to go. It's dangerous here."

"Where are we?"

"Never mind. Just stay here and you'll be all right. I'll be angry if I come back and find you gone!"

"Where are you going?"

"To find my friends. You stay put! There are things I don't dare broadcast." He climbed out over the pots and through the brick arch into the open air. "Don't call any Teachers. *They* won't give you any name . . . they won't tell you what you're supposed to do!" He grinned back at me and disappeared down the slope.

I sat there, quite happy for a while. It was quiet there, no one was chasing me for once, anyway, the Boy had ordered me to stay . . . there was no reason to call the Teachers yet. Then I thought of that Teacher I'd killed. It worried me for a while, but then I thought how that little Boy had killed so many, that twelve that I saw; I could hand him over, surely they'd forgive my one?

I got pretty drowsy in that kiln, there wasn't anything to do and for a while I enjoyed that. I might have gone to sleep then, I got like that sometimes when the tubes had hit me and there was nothing to do.

It was late when I sat up. The brickwork at the door had turned rosy in the sunset, the sky was darkening to the east. It'd been too long, I had to go and do something. I could never wait for long without I had to go and do something, if I didn't I got really low and felt useless. I started to wonder what it was all for, began to think about not having a name. What I usually did at times like that was to go and walk around. Make a trek, go a few hundred miles with Wolf, visit new Streets, go looking for the Great Robot. Not that I ever expected to meet it, but they used to say you could stop it, if you found it early enough. You were supposed to know it by a dog, a dog always knows a robot, even if it is disguised. That's why I got Wolf, to smell the Great Robot if I ever meet it. I sometimes thought that maybe that was what I was for, to stop the Great Robot, it was a Purpose I gave myself, that and the Preaching. But mostly I thought it was all a fable, like about the Saver.

When I started wondering what things were for I climbed out of the kiln and went out the way the Boy had gone.

The clearing was just like the one we'd left. Perhaps the Speaker was set a few yards to the left, maybe the plane wreck was a little more decayed. The Cottage there was like the other one before the bombs. I still had that weird feeling of having gone back in time. I don't know, I thought maybe the Corps could do things like that. Compared with the people on the Streets they were god-men. I stared at the Cottage until it started to get dark and it was the same no matter how I looked.

I went down to look the place over from close in. My dog wasn't anxious to go that way, perhaps he was thinking about the cat. When we got there it was still the same, but this time I couldn't open the door. I still couldn't see in the windows, if anything they were more opaque, as if the place was shut up. There was mud in front of the door and it was quite smooth. I thought for a moment that the Boy couldn't have gone that way, but then I remembered the fly-belt. When I walked across the mud I didn't leave any footprints either, and that was funny too. By then it was nearly dark and I was pretty full of tubes, so who could tell anyway? I washed my hands of it. You can't understand everything, you can't expect it all to be reasonable.

I wasn't going to stay there all night. I had a walk coming on, it was time I took another look for the Great Robot. Anyway, it only took a few hours for the Machines to get a fix on you, all the personal records are connected up in one place, maybe they could even predict where you wanted to go before you knew yourself. I had to keep moving, or they'd soon have the Teachers after me.

I made Wolf happy and went across the clearing and into the woods. There was a fence just inside the trees. There hadn't been at the other place. It took ten minutes to make up my mind, but then I crossed it quite easily.

Maybe it was just a token, a symbol. I went on through the trees.

It got colder first and then I noticed the smell of burning. It seemed everywhere. After a while I could smell cordite too and there were places where all the trees had shed their green leaves and they were lying like rotten slush, ankle deep on the ground. Once there was a low, wet clearing where some optimist had planted rice and that was rotten too.

I came through a place where there were burn marks on the trees from explosions and then I stepped out on to a ridge above the usual sort of country. I could see an apron around the nearest Street shine wet through the darkness.

All the way down the slope there were rocks shoving up through the turf and there seemed to be Speakers and Dispensers about the place as if they'd rained. I counted a set every ten yards. Every hundred or hundred and twenty yards there was a sort of round, stone building. They had paths leading up to them. I went towards the nearest one to see what it was.

I must have gone too close because someone gave a shout and loosed off at me with a machine rifle. You could tell it was a rifle because it was so quick and I could hear the bullets striking four hundred yards behind me, there was that small stab of flame you get with cordite too, that and hardly any smoke at all.

He missed me, of course, so I went back up a little and got behind one of the rocks. After a while the rifle man forgot about me and exchanged some shooting with someone in another building. There was quite a little battle there for a few minutes, practically all the towers joined in. I lay still while the bullets went over my head. When the firing stopped I picked my way down to the Street. A rifle was a thing I'd always wanted. I never got one.

When I was near enough I could see people standing about down there. I tightened my bandage, got Wolf's handle and went on.

They were all facing each other. The smell of the place was fear, you could have cut it with a knife. Even the music was hard and full of menace, the air seemed to taste of it. You could understand about those forts up the hill, a family in each maybe, or a clan, crowded and fearful in there. You couldn't tell how many might crush into a place like that. I wouldn't have liked it in there.

When I turned back to the apron a couple of people had been edging towards me. When I faced them they froze. I turned away again for a moment and when I looked back they were closer. It was like a game. After a moment Wolf noticed it too and growled.

"I'm a poor blind man . . ." I said. "Is anyone there?"

The nearest one jumped at me. I caught a flash of a razor and let him have the top barrel of my gun before he got too close. I'd loaded that barrel with magnesium dust. I got that from the Teachers too, I used it sometimes at night. It made a good, frightening flash.

The glare lit all their wild faces. The one I fired at took the charge across his chest and went down in a heap.

They all stood still. The wadding glowed red as it blew across the apron. There was an outbreak of firing back on the surrounding hills. All the people looked at me very carefully, we didn't give the hurt man a second look. Hell, I felt bad about that too, but you've got to show you can handle yourself.

After a while the man I'd shot groaned and dragged himself off. I stood there wishing the lights would come on, but there wasn't any hope of that, someone had shot them all. There was broken glass under all the poles.

"Pretty good," a voice sneered from the top of the gantry. "That was very nasty. Well up to your standard, Candy Man!" It was the Boy. I could tell by the voice. I could see him up there, absurdly small against the sky. I concentrated and pointed my head at the gantry stem.

"That you? That my friend K?"

"No. No friend to you! You've got to learn not to mess me, Candy Man!"

I walked a bit towards him. It was long range for my gun. I liked to keep my friends in range.

"I owe you a little something," he said. "Oh, yes, they were really badly burned . . . they had to put back a new set. But it hurt . . . it hurt! I nearly died while I killed those Teachers . . ."

I wondered if it'd be better to make it back to the

shadows. There was something coming, something big. Lights . . . dim ones . . . and the noise of an engine too.

"You'll pay for it, Candy. Yes, you will, indeed you will! I'll make you pay for it now!" The lights that were coming hit him for a moment. It was the Boy all right. You could see every line on his face, every furrow of his scowl, that unpleasant grin he had all the time. It was no time to plead friendship. It was a time to run, it really was. That Boy had the hate and fear of that country all over his face.

He pulled a big pistol out of a holster clip on his belt. He weighed it in his hand, as if he was letting me see it . . . he was smiling in my face.

"Break legs and send for Teachers?" He aimed at my feet. "That's the way to do it, isn't it? Answer!"

"Yes . . . poor, blind . . ." The first charge smashed into the naked concrete a yard to my left. I felt chips of the stuff bite at my legs.

"How will you get new genitals when I burn yours up? Have you the facilities I have?" He was shouting over the roar of the approaching motor but he didn't seem to notice it. That thing that was coming—a hoverer it was—came on to the apron. The noise lowered a little. It bowed down its head, landed and the people began to climb in. All the time they carefully watched each other, tried not to turn their backs. They weren't looking at the Boy and me. To tell the truth I wasn't watching them much either.

"Blind!" He was laughing over the engine noise. He still didn't seem to have noticed the hoverer. "You're not blind! Say you're not blind, Candy!" His second charge smashed in on my right. I got chips up that leg too. Then his head went back to laugh some more and I saw my chance.

I brought up my gun and fired the second barrel at him. It was almost too far, but what else could I do? I don't know why he ignored my gun the way he did. Perhaps he thought I'd fired both barrels at the man I'd hurt.

Only part of the charge hit him and that was Luck. It was in the face and the little wire tails layed open his cheek and showed his mandible as neat as a whistle. It was a Lucky freak, the charge was pretty near spent.

There was a clarity in my vision right then. As if I was right on the crest of a tube. I got like that when I was in danger, or sometimes when I'd hurt someone. Anyway, I saw it all. I saw that pale, perfect cheek open up. I saw him drop his pistol and clap his hand up. I saw the pistol jerk back into its clips, I saw the wadding hit him on his shoulder. There wasn't much time between them. It was slow, there was hardly time to calculate. It was like that—I had the vision then all right—the Luck!

He tottered on the gantry. His hands over his face and then the wadding hit him and he fell into the Street. He didn't fall far. The airstream hit him, he steadied and then began to come up. He had one of those fly-belts and he was using that. Even then he had that pistol out and he was looking to kill me.

I ran to the hoverer. I got a foot in just as the door was closing and it opened again for me. I fell on to the floor, someone reached for me but I clubbed his hand with my gun barrel and maybe broke his wrist for him. They left me alone then and I concentrated on loading my gun.

The motors gunned and the hoverer lifted its front and drove off fast across the apron. I didn't look back.

That hoverer smelled of urine. It was in a bad condition, the lights weren't even working properly, when it blew its horn you could hardly hear it. The windows were scarred where bullets had hit them, in places they were still there, embedded in white impact circles. The metal was dented too. Someone had used a heavier weapon about half way back and the seats were ripped where the explosion had come in. Some blood had dried old and black on the floor.

Part of the skirt seemed to be missing, so the machine bottomed sometimes. When that happened a crack that ran right across the floor opened and exhaust fumes came through. If you looked you could see blue flame coming from the rotaries down there. Petrol motors were OK, in their way, but they didn't use things like that in the old days. The units on the Teachers' chairs were better. Nowadays there's hardly the skill to make an internal combustion engine, I didn't remember seeing a new one.

When the hoverer bottomed the passengers all jerked up and felt at their weapons. They were all young, all of them

47

. . . twelve to fifteen, all boys. No forehead scars and there weren't any names around their necks.

We all sat separate, hunched up. Some were trying to catch some sleep without the rest of us knowing. When I studied them they all looked like babies waiting to be born. Foetal position, they used to say you spent your first nine months trying to get born and the rest of your life trying to get back to that warm safety. I know I feel like that sometimes, in those days I felt like it a lot.

We all sat in the stink of ammonia, in the cold draughts and the half light, the batter of the open exhausts. Two hours went by and we were still sitting in our small, opposite corners, watching each other's reflections in the dark glass, watching while the night went on slowly.

I started wondering where we were headed. We were sure going somewhere. We didn't wander from Street to Street the way hoverers usually did. Nobody seemed to be using the machine to get from one Street to another. Not that people did much, the hoverers just went on and on, but mostly they went empty. When we did occasionally stop at a Street no one got off, people just got on. When five more boys got on at the seventh stop it dawned on me.

We were on the way to the Rites! My stomach turned to lead and I started to shiver. I didn't want to go to any Rites. I sure didn't want to go near *there*!

But I was going. After all that time I was going whether I liked it or not. I had to get off quick!

I didn't dare get out at any of the Streets. The hoverer only stopped there and when it did sometimes the lights brightened. If the Boy should show up, I wouldn't have a chance the second time, not on an apron, not under the lights.

If there'd been a driver I'd have used my gun and made him stop. But there was only a computer and they won't listen to reason. I couldn't find any way I could get out of the thing. The door was locked while we were moving. I couldn't get at the computer, it was all covered with plastic armour and it had 'DANGER, HIGH VOLTAGE' stamped on it in twelve different places. The cables and conduits leading to the servos were all just the same.

I took a couple of small inspection panels up out of the

floor, but someone else had been there first and smashed whatever had been behind. I put them back carefully—they were Teachers' property after all—and stood up. I thought about the Rites and caught some more of the fear everybody had. The hoverer bucketed on. One of the boys stood up to urinate on the swaying floor. I wished I'd done what I was told and stayed in the kiln.

I went upstairs to see if I could hide there, but there was no hope of that. How can you hide in an observation dome? The seats were thicker but you couldn't get underneath them. Far to the west I could see those tower forts burning.

I leaned over one of the seats and took a tube. Right then it seemed to me that maybe that was really why I was there. Really like maybe that was what I was for, why I existed, just to take tubes to make me happy because I was worried.

There were hills all around us. Dark hills lit with burning, ragged trees reaching across the sky line. As we went on there were more and more fires, the hills flickered with separate explosions. It started to rain. The front lights showed little of where we were going, but it was all nasty. I thought how I'd be glad to even face the Rites to leave that country, if I lived there.

Some of the armour above my head had sprung apart and the rain started dripping cold on my neck.

"Yes!" said the Boy in my ear. "Yes, much better you're going where you're going. Much better you can only half see the way. You couldn't take all the truth!" I must have been thinking aloud and he'd been listening.

I whirled. My gun swung with me. The Boy was there all right, but outside the dome, flying there on his belt. Keeping pace—it was like a nightmare. He carefully pointed that big pistol of his at me. When I ducked he lowered it and laughed.

"I can always find you," he said. "Every time I can always find you!" He'd put a sucker against the glass, it connected back to him and now he was talking through it.

"You can't get me in here!" I wasn't so sure of that, but the thing that was sure was that I couldn't get at him, anyway, I didn't see how I could survive another encounter. He laughed again, he still laughed a lot, he'd had his jaw fixed.

One or two of the boys downstairs looked up—there was a crack in that floor too—but they soon looked away again. They had trouble and fear enough of their own to care about.

We went on like that for another twenty miles. Him out there laughing and me trying to pretend he wasn't. It was terrible, the red glow of fire, the explosions, and him laughing in the rain. The hair straggled across his face, his shirt wet and clinging, the knee breeches and dainty cloth belt stained black with water.

"I'll be seeing you again! When you least expect it, in some familiar place where you feel safe. When you're happy one day and think you've won!" He moved in even closer, I saw the rain bead on his face. "I'll come and kill you then. I'll always find you, Candy! I always will! Where you going to hide, Candy Man?"

He was laughing again, sneering at me, smiling all the time. In close I'd seen the tear on his cheek was clipped together and smeared with something shiny. It looked almost healed already but how he could talk with a shot up jaw I don't know . . .

Maybe he'd used that toothpick somehow . . . but by then I'd had two tubes so I didn't care. I just wished he'd come in and get it settled, or just go away. On two tubes I knew I was more than a match for any Boy. He was soaked, he must have really hated me to stay out there like that. He got the sucker, put it on his belt and backed off into the murk.

When he'd gone I remembered the crack between the sheets of armour. I got my knife in there and twisted the blade. I managed to shift it a quarter of an inch. The water ran in and the wind buffeted my ears. The hoverer was only making twenty miles an hour, if I could have got it open I could have dropped down easy and not hurt a thing.

It wasn't like that. I only broke my knife and cut my thumb. When I'd stopped that bleeding and I looked up we were going under this arch made of a million coloured lights. I dropped everything, checked my gun and pushed it inside my rubbers to hide it.

We'd come to the Rites. We were at that terrible place and it was too late to get out even if I could. It was too late to run from there, once you're committed to the Machines you just have to go on.

CHAPTER SIX

THE HOVERER MOVED in slowly through the dancing, surging people. It was confusion to look at—all the shining lights and the wet apron. I tried the door again, but it was still no good.

Up ahead you could see the lights of the Rites ground proper. On either side the hoverers were drawing up in rows, they were never there for long, the whole place moved with their stopping and starting . . . the boys pouring out of them. The girls' place was somewhere else. You weren't allowed in there, of course.

Our hoverer kept on nosing in looking for a place to stop. There were machines pulling out all the time but when we got near a slot some other hoverer would always get there first. The Rites went on for ever. They were continuous, they never stopped, they'd been going on since time started. It was just the people that kept changing . . . right then all I wanted was to get off.

We made it in the end. The hoverer found a place and we climbed out into the roaring rain, the cacophony of the shouting and music. The boys went one way and I went the other. I never heard music louder than then.

I was desperate. Hell! I mean, I had to get out of there! It was all wrong for me. I was *worried*. I didn't have any right, I had no business in there. I didn't want any brain trimming either—even if those boys did. It was just a question of time before they got me and found out who I was.

It was hot and hard to breathe between the hoverers, the

rain came down like rods. Those clattering motors pumped out a fog of fumes. Twice I nearly got run over when machines swung out. I ducked under window level and went scuttling away trying to be invisible. There was only one way out and that was under the light arch we'd come in under. I made that way.

There was a centre concourse between garish ranks of stalls that ran up to the arch. People made a sort of living there selling Luck charms and pastries, drinks and candy, stuff like that, to the boys. Mostly the stall people were those who'd funked the Rites when they had come to them. They were a poor lot, I suppose the Teachers tolerated them because they were all in one place. That's where I'd be if I didn't get away and the Teachers didn't get me. I could always sell floss, if it came to that.

There were many lights there too, like on the Streets, on standards, each surrounded by its halo of rain. The music was loudest there, every lamp post had its Speaker. They went on beyond the arch too.

When I got nearer the entrance I had to come close to the concourse, so I crept in behind the stalls. There was no pavement there, I was splashing in the mud, moving all the time to that flashing bright arch and the safety outside. I pulled down the fastening on my rubbers and shifted the butt of my gun to where I could get at it. It was better now I was going somewhere, better to be out of that hoverer and my own master and a direction to go in. At least if I got killed it'd be in my own way, as far as it ever might be, anyway.

Seventy yards from the arch I hit the inner perimeter. It was one of those special Teachers' fences all hung with neon signs about things you mustn't do. It was only a few strands of rust-thin wire, but it was a Teachers' fence so you couldn't cut it or force through or anything. I suddenly wondered why I'd got my gun ready. I mean, I knew there'd be Teachers on the arch. I wondered if it could be that I was getting ready to shoot at another Teacher, kill one perhaps.

I felt cold then. I mean, I wasn't any Boy that could kill a dozen and not turn a hair. I went through the soggy grass along the fence to where there was an awning that was drumming in the wind, splashing rain under the million lights. The apron dazzled me, it was like jewels. I went past the notices hung on the wire, all the time hating the dark things I couldn't think about, the things that sent me against Teachers. There were three Teachers behind paper strewn desks under the awning.

"Yes?" said the first Teacher. His mask glinted rain in the coloured lights. It was beautiful.

"A mistake . . ." The heavy drops thudded on my shoulders. "Sir . . . I'm blind. I shouldn't be here."

"Ah . . ." The Teacher had a severe voice, but he spoke kindly. The Teachers were marvellous. My heart went out in gratitude.

"So you've changed your mind?" said the second. They were marvellous but they didn't always understand very quickly.

"No . . . I can't go on. I'm blind!" I pointed up to my bandage. At last he nodded.

"Ah. Yes. But I'm not sure we can let you out again as easily as that." I got that sickening vision of those bloody legs just spinning up against the sky. I prayed nothing would happen.

"You should really *follow through*!" he went on. "When you decide to do a thing you should do it. Name?"

"Let him," said one of the others. "Poor blind man! What can he have seen? They're supposed to be Lucky, you know."

"Well . . ."

"Let him go." The first Teacher nodded. I took my hand out of my rubbers. It was going to be all right.

"You go quickly. We won't remember anything about it."

I walked as quickly as I dared through the arch and on to the apron beyond. It was unbelievable. Things were going right.

I thought about having a tube to celebrate but then I decided I didn't need it. There were seven roads leading away, all with those lights. I took the middle one and tried to keep from singing.

At first there was a forest of lights, but as I got further and the roads diverged they thinned out. I hadn't made two hundred yards when the light I was under exploded and I was showered by broken glass. When I looked ahead the Boy was there.

He hovered twenty yards ahead and to my left. He'd just shot out the light, his pistol was still glowing violet and steaming a little.

"Here, Candy. Over here! I want to see your face." He beckoned me with the gun and I turned towards him.

"Candy! Candy, I'm going to give you a choice. I'll cripple you *now*, send for the Teachers, then tell them who you are and what you've done. I'll do that . . . or . . . you can walk back to the Rites, fail them, and get your mind burned out. You're too stupid for the Corps, they'll burn you out . . ." He paused, ran the pistol up his thigh. He didn't seem very angry, but he was sure soaked from the rain. "I might still want to kill you . . . when you're too stupid to know why . . . or again, I might not . . ."

I couldn't get out my gun. I didn't have a chance. There was a long silence. The rain spattered on the road. I thought how I'd rather die than get the burns, how I'd try for my gun anyway. I didn't convince myself though, not in time.

"Too late! Too late!" That pistol pointed at my stomach. "You lose the choice! Try to learn to make your mind up, Candy! You go to the Rites! I'll come to you again when you're stupid! Move!" He aimed very deliberately between my eyes. I really didn't have a choice then, he'd made it an order. All I could do was go back.

I was miserable walking back that big lonely road. The Boy was there all the time. He hovered behind me in the gloom, I could see him on the edge of the lights. I thought how those Teachers might know me when I got back. Everything was in the records. I wondered if I'd be Lucky the second time and I didn't see how I could be.

"Good!" said the first Teacher when I got there. "So glad you came back. It really is best to finish what you start!"

And that was it. I walked back in just like that. They always used to say it was hardest getting out.

The Boy didn't let me hang about in the stalls. I tried to lose myself there, but every time I slowed up he'd appear at my elbow to drive me on again. I had to go . . . all the time my mind was racing for a way out and finding nothing.

It was a nightmare. All those yelling, smelly boys whipping up their spirits before they went through the second arch, the din of the music, the mud, all those boys lower than animals. There were Teachers there too, standing on plinths, urging everyone on. I could see the second arch ahead and all the time getting bigger.

Then I stopped. Right there, right on the threshold I could go no further. I was shaking, angry at the wrong of it. I shouldn't be going in there. There was no Purpose in it.

"Good riddance!" The Boy put his foot in the small of my back and shoved me staggering through. I heard the barriers click behind me. I was in. I knew I'd never get back that way. Almost the last thing I heard was the Boy laughing.

It was different in there. The things outside, the lights and the music and even the Boy's laughter were muted. They went on, but they faded down, they stopped being real and then ended. It was like dying.

Then there was a white maze in front of me. It was brilliant with light. When I looked up for the sun there wasn't any, just a hard blue sky. That maze stretched ahead, brilliant in light and dark, totally without colour and very clean.

I took a moment to try and think. I saw the maze was bigger than it looked. Under my feet it was lines on the floor, then, on a little, there were small walls and pretty soon they were knee high. After that they went on growing until they were as high as mountains. Everything got bigger as it went away, it was very hard to tell distances. Then I had to go forward, I *had* to, it was the only thing to do.

I picked a likely looking path and walked down it. Pretty soon the path roofed over and I was in a tunnel. I found a couple of dead ends, but I never had far to go back.

For a long time the light was just as bright as ever but it changed and got darker. Somehow it didn't though, if you can guess what I mean; the light was blue and it was white, but it was dark as well. I had a sense that there were a lot of vibrations there that I couldn't see. About then I took a tube and started wondering how long I'd been going. I lost my sense of time altogether in the end and then all I could do was count the empty tubes and wonder if I'd lost any. It was all subjective in there, even for me.

After that I remember climbing up narrow, dark tunnels. Then again, sometimes, it was going down, and a lot of the time I didn't know which it was. The floor was slippery, then rough, then sticky. I clawed and crawled over pebbles, over yielding surfaces like women, I was pressed and squeezed and nearly suffocated. All the time I was going higher or deeper or east or west, I just didn't know and I had to keep on because the tunnel was closing behind me. It was like being inside something living and I didn't like it much.

When at last I had three empty tubes—which made it thirty-six hours, more or less—I got out of that part. I fell through the floor into a room full of people who looked just like me. I screamed and they all screamed back.

Somehow my gun was in my hands and I fired it. All the guns in the world went off. Five hundred Candy Men all pointed red fire and smoke at me. The sound was one great crash that echoed for ever.

Then I heard glass fall and one of me had disappeared. Only mirrors, we were only mirrors. I laughed and we all laughed. When the sound came back at me it sounded mad, so I stopped. After a moment the mirrors did too.

There were more miles of mirrors then. I walked on through them, looking about me and feeling worried. Those mirrors were every size and shape, set at all angles, far and near, on the floors and ceilings, the walls too, if there were any. Mostly there was only a floor, just a floor and that infinite variety of mirrors. Once in a while there'd be a distorting one, convex or concave. I'd look at my grotesque belly or my enormous head and that'd be all right. In a funny way they seemed to mean more than the natural images, the endless sameness of the others. I dragged on looking for caricatures, looking for something different, hoping for a change.

Then I started seeing things. I thought I saw the sea first. Not like those shores near the cascades where all the rotting things wash up, but something better. Slatey green grey cliffs with thin veins of quartz in them, sand and sea shells, then sun and cornfields on low cliffs and headlands. I thought I saw all that in a mirror, but when I looked again it was gone and all that was there was my pale and dirty face.

"Haven't you noticed?" said the Boy.

I looked up. There he was reflected behind me. I turned quickly and he was reflected there too.

"Really," he said, "you should have noticed. You could lose the Rites for a thing like that." He laughed when he said that. It was as if he was teasing me, but *gently*. Not like before.

Then I saw what it was I should have noticed. Those reflections. They should have all been different . . . but they were all the same. Myself all seen from the same angle . . . even the ones overhead all showed the same thing, me full faced, looking stupid and surprised. The Boy was behind me in them all, smiling and shaking his head.

"You should have stayed in the kiln. Look at the trouble you'd have saved."

I started feeling around for my gun. That Boy—you didn't know how he'd be from one minute to the next. He'd had his face fixed, I could see that. The clips were gone and there was no scar. I wondered if he'd forgiven me again, I allowed he might have, he could change like the wind.

"I suppose you'd better come through," he said. "I'll want to keep an eye on you. I'll look after you, Candy Man. I believe we can use you, no matter what the others say." He was looking hard at me and he was picking his teeth again.

"Come in," he said.

I was so surprised I did that. I walked forward and stepped right through that mirror and it didn't hurt at all.

"Dodgson's Law," said the Boy. "It takes a special mirror." I don't know what he meant.

We were inside that Cottage. Or rather another just like it. I looked around. The pots were still there, fired now, finished, all shiny with glaze. There were noises out at the back, that Potter was there, he had a tray of pots beside him. He picked them up one by one, he held each pot up to the light, turning it, looking at it. Then he deliberately put it on the floor beside him and hit it with a hammer. He kept on doing that, all the time we were in there was punctuated with the noise of breaking pottery.

"Take it off," said the Boy. "Take it off. Take off the bandage. "You can see—can't you?" I hesitated. "Go on, you're out of it here, when you go back you can put it on again. I won't tell."

"What's that noise?" I jerked my head towards the Potter.

"Oh . . . *him*!" The Boy shrugged. "He's trying to make the 'perfect shape'. He thinks he'll know it if he makes it! He doesn't think about anything else. Take it off, or I'll dump you in the Rites . . ."

I unwound the cloth. The light came flooding in. Honey and amber, the place was a haze of gold. It was warm, beautiful, like on the top of a tube.

"You've got nice eyes . . . a pity to waste them."

"I still can't see . . ." I didn't trust the Boy, of course. I fell over a chair to try and convince him. I don't know if he believed me. He just went to the wall where the dials were, he bent into the humming screens.

"Now then." The Cottage blinked. Came and went. Fluttered in its reality. "Come on!"

The Boy made for the far wall. There was a door there now. I looked and there were two others that hadn't been there before. The Potter broke another pot. There were some extra windows too.

"Come on!" The Boy walked across the room and opened the door, then he came back and pointed me at it. It was blue out there and sunshine streamed in. It was all sea blue and greenness, in the distance there was yellow waving corn. It was like I'd seen in the mirror. I hesitated . . . it looked so good. All I could think of was that it had to be time travel.

"Come on! You liked it when I showed you before!" He stepped out into the sunshine, on to the bright grass. I looked at the light on his hair, the miraculous bright clean detail of his clothes. He shrugged. "You come on when you're ready. I'll be waiting."

I still didn't go. All my experience was against it. Another pot exploded under the Potter's hammer. I was wondering if I still had the Boy fooled about my blindness, after the mirrors and things. He said he knew I could see, but I didn't know whether to believe that or not. It was confusing. I thought I could hear the gentle lap of the sea, somewhere there was a cow lowing.

"Come on!" The Boy's voice was getting fainter. I decided I couldn't miss it, maybe it'd be my only chance to get into that paradise out there. And anyway, it was a way out of the Rites, a way out without getting my brain burned.

I stood in the door frame looking out. It was a river. Broad and flat, rich, gentle hills on either side. Five miles on there were two headlands and the sea between them. The mouth was a mile wide there, nearer it was much more. One of the headlands was crowned with a fine looking castle, nearer a pink and white town rose up out of the water. There were sailing boats everywhere. It was the middle of the morning and there were orange and brown butterflies with white flecks on their wings. Honey bees murmured.

Something smashed into the door frame. Burning splinters twisted past my eyes. The Boy was twenty yards off firing at me.

"Treacherous!" he yelled. "I've got you now, Candy!"

He was shaking with rage. The scar was livid on his cheek. He held his weapon in both hands, trying to steady it at me. He couldn't. He brought shattered melting guttering down across my shoulders. I smelled the burning of my rubbers and woke up. I yelped and fell over myself getting back into the Cottage.

I didn't wait. That Boy was coming. I crossed the room in a bound to the door there, the one I'd come through. It wouldn't open.

I turned back to try and shoot the Boy. Then I remembered my gun wasn't loaded. A charge came through the open door, smashed some pots for the Potter. He looked up, frowned. I couldn't see what odds it made. Then I went through the window feet first in a shower of broken glass and broken wood and landed back in the mirrors.

I chased my echoing footsteps into the flapping images of a thousand running Candy Men until I could run no more. All the time I expected to be blasted. All the time I thought that Boy would jump out in front of me. All the time I was worried, but nothing like that happened.

It was a sort of hell. A crushing disappointment. To see that lovely place, then get chased out again and into the Rites. I thought it was that Boy; just setting me up and torturing me with things I couldn't have. That place . . . that paradise . . . I could have lived there and done nothing, never wondered what on earth I was for.

CHAPTER SEVEN

A LONG WHILE later—about half of time it felt like—but I still couldn't tell how long, I got out of the mirrors and it wasn't so bad. I hated it in there, I liked to tell the time.

A plain. Dead flat, gigantic, still brilliantly lit, surrounded by the mirror maze, glinting and deceptive, an image forest. There were buildings further ahead. In the shifting distance where the hot air stirred I could see bright domes, coloured tents and shining aluminium structures. Banners flew there, bright balloons marked the spot, I caught the flash of circling doves.

I set off to walk towards them and there was suddenly music at my feet. In close I could see the plain wasn't sand like I first thought, but something special. Small, white, bone shapes, all individual, all shaped and modelled like toy bones, the ground was covered with little fantastic sculptured things. Like sand, I suppose, like sand and fragments of shells, but different, bigger grained, *different*, somehow more perfect, like they'd all been designed. When you walked on them they struck little sounds and notes, the music I'd heard. Once in a while there'd be a flurry of breeze and that sounded beautiful too. I started towards the tent again and after a while a machine came and raked the stuff flat where my feet had been. I watched it for a while, but it didn't threaten me so I went on.

Nearer the buildings the going got firmer and two hundred yards from the first dome my feet didn't sink at all. Grass started to grow up through the sand and it became silent. There were other people too. I couldn't see them from further out, but now I saw them coming in from all angles. The music started again, not like the sand, but the proper sounds, like outside. There wasn't any shouting, everyone was quiet, the music seemed calm and without threat. I started to feel better, it wasn't like in the mirrors and it certainly wasn't like on the Streets.

There were more and more boys coming in all the time, coming out of the light haze round the edge of the plain. Teachers wheeled out to meet them, spoke to everybody, told them all where they had to go.

It was comforting. I had trouble remembering that the Teachers were after me. Even if they weren't it still wouldn't have done for me on the plain. I knew what it was like in the Corps, I'd seen what it was like in their world. That Boy had shown me before he tried to kill me. I just wanted to get back *there*—I *had* to. I started wondering if I could possibly pass the Rites. I stopped and took a tube before I went to meet the Teachers.

"Welcome to the Rites!" said the Teacher that came to me. "This is where it starts! THE GLORIES! HUMANITY! The way to the private and secret places . . . the way to join the CORPS! This is the introduction! A glimpse of rewards, the way of living!"

"Suppose I fail?" If there was one thing I hated it was enthusiasm. It was too easily wrong, too *human.*

"Then we'll see you neither remember nor care." He looked hard at me. "You shouldn't consider that . . . but I suppose you're older than the others . . ." He couldn't see my false scars because I'd dragged my hair forward.

"What about the maze? What about the mirrors? Wasn't that the start?"

"Ah . . . you had the *mirrors.*" He tapped a note on his keyboard. I had the feeling of having given something away, of somehow having exposed myself.

"So?"

"Not everyone gets the same. Some get monsters or women. Dreams of visions of greatness, dwarfs and midgets, weird adventures with scientific apparatus. It varies for people. It all means *something* . . . it's all recorded, the maze your mind projects is written down."

I asked him what he meant but he wouldn't say. I wondered if I'd imagined it all in there, if I'd imagined the Boy and what had happened. To have seen heaven and then to find you'd dreamed it! Hell could be like that. I didn't say anything about the Boy. A bit of paper came clicking out of the arm rest on the Teacher's chair.

"Egocentric . . ." I heard him murmur. "Self mania. Onan as his philosopher?" He turned back to me. "Did you see tunnels . . . soft insides? It all means something . . . nothing about guns? Important doors? Do you feel threatened by the younger generation? No girls? Your mother . . . views of the sea? Rivers?"

I said no. He stopped questioning me then. Maybe all that stuff wasn't important, maybe it all meant nothing.

"Rites first," he said. "This way." We crossed over the smooth turf between the bright tents and aluminium domes standing on their aprons.

It was all so clean there. All in clear pastel colours, the small bushes were closely trimmed, the flowers seemed to smell of antiseptic. There were banks of fountains beyond the tents, a dozen barbered trees stood behind them, the music was very soft.

"Of course, the lower grades don't even get through their mazes." My Teacher took me by the arm and pointed me towards the first of the domes. "We frighten most of them into turning back. The things the Machines take from their deepest minds, the hidden fears there, their greatest hopes. We bombard them with the fears, we trounce their hopes. When they turn back they fail . . ."

That explained the mirrors, I wondered if the Boy I'd seen was like that. Seeming to accept and help me, then rejecting me with charges from his pistol.

The Rites tests in the first dome were straightforward. Basically they were jig-saw puzzles, but three dimensional. There was nothing you had to *know* anything for, the answers were in the pieces and they gave you them. There was nothing to it. I was surprised when some of the boys failed.

The Teachers grabbed them at once and dragged them off to get their brains burned before they were put back on the Streets. I went quickly past the scuffles and out the other side of the dome.

When I got back into the sun my Teacher was waiting for me. He kept me standing there while one of those instruction slips came ticking out of the arm of his chair. He read them, then looked up at me.

"Good . . . very good." I couldn't see what expression his face had, but I heard the surprise and pleasure in his voice. "You've really done well. Quick too!" As I said, there was nothing hard about those Rites, all the answers were intrinsic; I just wished he hadn't sounded so surprised.

"Come on." He led me briskly through the succeeding Rites tests. Every time he got more and more excited. "A Corps man!" I heard him say to himself. "One in twenty thousand!" He began to call to other Teachers and they'd leave their boys to come and look at me. I got to like it, it was good to please them, but it was like being a prize specimen and not a man at all. That's what the Rites were for really, to find the good specimens.

My Teacher began getting more and more instructions out of his chair. Then he'd turn his lead face to me and ask me questions about where I was born and who my father was, what connections I had.

"I wish you'd remember," he said once. "I wish you'd really try, it'd help you if you've got good antecedents . . . ?" I tried but I couldn't help him, it was all too long ago.

The Rites kept on. I remember one where you had to pass between two drums that revolved and flailed chains across the path between them. You could just about do it if you were nimble and timed it right. I saw two boys go through that way but I did it by walking down the top of one of the drum covers. My Teacher was delighted. He said no one had thought of that for hundreds of years. I smiled and tried to look modest but intelligent too.

It wasn't all fun, there was a lot of instruction. Interesting things like how birds flew and fish swam. They said how engines worked and about etiquette and what you should enjoy. There were long, dramatic lectures about how it was the only thing to pass the Rites; how it was almost as good to be a Teacher if you couldn't quite make it into Exploration Corps.

"Not that *you* have to worry about *that*!" My Teacher clutched my arm, whispered up close to my ear from behind his lead mask. "*You're* a Corps man if I ever saw one!"

They taught us useful things, too, about war cholera and pulmonary anthrax, how to cure and use them. They said where to shoot a man so that he was only maimed and you had time to question him. In one place there was a picture of a man nailed up on a gallows and someone who was sticking a spear into him.

My Teacher said how that was an act of mercy showing how you should always put a man out of his misery when you'd got your answers. Then he gave me a phial of something called 'paste of Rocky Mountain spotty fever' and said it was a special present for his best pupil. He was pretty pleased with himself, anyone would have thought it was him doing the work and not me.

There were questions every two hours. After every examination there were boys grabbed and carried off to to get the burns. Mind, those questions were difficult. The answers weren't in them, you had to know things.

It was all right for me, somehow I always seemed to know all the answers. I hadn't ever suspected I knew things like that, the questions would come and my stomach would turn to water because I didn't have the answer and then I would. The right words I hadn't known would come welling up and it'd be all right except that I was trembling all over.

After every session my Teacher would get the results out of his chair and embrace me, shake my hands. I was surprised I'd taken in so much without knowing it. I was glad when the questioning was finally over and we were standing outside the last dome, close to the fountains.

"Well," I said. "What's next? When do I get my name?" I hadn't considered it when it had started, it hadn't seemed possible, but it looked as if I was going to

64

pass the Rites. It looked as if the Boy had done me a favour after all.

"You're so *good*," said the Teacher. "One in five hundred thousand. I can hardly believe it! It seems impossible that you could come out of the Streets in this age!" His chair arm clicked and he got one of those slips again. He read it, then looked up at me. When he spoke his voice was hushed.

"You are *special* . . . the Machine has noticed your results! A great honour. For me as well as you . . ."

I wasn't so keen on that. Sooner or later the Deep Machine would make the connections and know I was Candy Man. Sooner or later it'd know I'd killed that Teacher and then I wouldn't last five minutes.

"What next?" I said quickly. "Let's get on!" If I could only get right through and get a name. It'd be OK then, they'd start a new record and Candy Man wouldn't come into it.

"Ah . . . yes . . . the Ladies. See how you get on here. Remember it's still part of the Rites." He led me past the fountains and into the other half of the Rites ground. On the way we passed the pens where the failures got the burns. There was a Street there and Whistlers to ship the stumbling boys out. The Teachers put them in a sort of crate where their heads were held in the right place. Then there was a flash of multiple beams focused into the boy's skull and he screamed and twisted once. When they let them out the boys walked quietly away; you could see the burn marks on their foreheads and they didn't struggle any more. One glimpse was enough for me. I walked quickly through the fountain spray and put it behind me.

"Don't worry!" said my Teacher when he caught up. "They wouldn't be happy on the Streets un-treated. You're all right. The rest is a formality." I just hoped they never found out who I was.

"Now then," he went on. "Basic biology. The last Rite." We'd come to the first of the tents on that side. I glimpsed boys moving there, each with his individual Teacher. They all seemed pretty pleased with themselves, they had a right to be. They'd passed; there weren't very many of them.

What was going on in that tent was nasty. The girls were

in there too and they were being mated to the boys. By numbers, by rote. The boys and girls came in from opposite ends and as they entered they drew a number. Then they found the matching number and that was their partner.

"You mustn't think of it on the Streets," said my Teacher. "There it's nasty, uncontrolled. That's why we don't let it happen, all that random fortune of chance mixing. How could the race remain great unless there is control of these things?"

"It happens sometimes, or where do *they* all come from?" I asked, but he just ignored me and went on with what he was saying.

"Perhaps you have already grasped the essential fact that man, until he passes the Rites, is only beastly, an animal?" I just grunted.

"You must *pass*. It's different here." He waved his hand into the tent. "You must bring yourself to do it. I see it must be an effort for a man like you, a potential Corps Man! You must! Where else do you think most of the Teachers come from? All Teachers do it once, it's not so bad! We know what happens on the Streets, but it's *different* here. All Teachers owe it to posterity to do it *once* . . . so that we need not draw on the Street people."

There was instruction first. The boys stood gravely round while there were lectures and demonstrations. They had a woman up on a plinth under a glass dome. As I watched she arched her back and laughed. She was all wired up, she was being recorded all the time.

"Our first demonstration," said my Teacher. He'd seen where I was looking, he studied my face. "It's all right, it's the Machine that's doing it. Look, you can watch it on the screens . . . every tiny pulse intimately recorded. See the dials? The white tiles and glass? There's no *contact* . . . nobody is enjoying it . . . it's not like the Streets. Everything is recorded, it's *all right*!"

I didn't say anything. I went on through the smell of antiseptic to where they had a man on the other side of the screen.

"You see it's hygienic. We separate the sexes . . . there's

plenty of light . . . no fumbling in the *dark*. Nothing *dirty* . . ."

I kept telling myself how you can't apply the usual rules to the superior orders, to science. I knew I shouldn't judge them. I asked myself how it was different from what I did on the Streets. But I couldn't compare them, I mean, I had to do it, I had a reason, I had to have my tubes.

"You look worried?" said my Teacher. "All right?"

"Yes!" Sometimes I lied, even to Teachers.

"It's all right. It's treated as *science*. All the reactions are metered." He looked thoughtful for a moment. "They do say that once it was all done in incubators and bottles. *Cleanly* with full control. It's another of those high things we've lost. We do the best we can. Come on, we must go to the practical bay."

There were some Lady Teachers in there. One of them had long blonde hair like a helmet and I never saw such a fat lady. The boys were joining them, searching about for whoever had drawn their lot. They didn't seem to be enjoying it much, but I don't suppose they necessarily had to.

"You wouldn't care to . . . ?"

"No!" He'd have to order me to do that. I strode on as quickly as I decently could and the Teacher had to trundle fast to catch me.

"No hurry. Some people find they enjoy it. You see those Lady Teachers? They keep coming back."

I didn't understand it and I didn't like it. I don't know why, things just shouldn't be like that between men and women. It was indecent, like vivisection.

I blundered out of that tent and into another where they were demonstrating childbirth and that was where I passed out. Man, but that shouldn't happen to a dog! It's not the sort of thing anyone like me should see.

I came round and they had me strapped into a Teacher's chair that had no wheels. They had electrodes on my head and I couldn't move a muscle.

"Ah!" said my Teacher when he saw I was awake. "I told you the Deep Machine was interested! While you were out orders came and I gave you the blood and gene tests.

67

The Machine said you should have the *Sleep*! They don't do that for everyone!"

My heart sank but I didn't have time to worry about it. He held a jug up to my mouth and I had to take a mouthful of the stuff in it. He didn't tell me to swallow so when he turned to check some dials I spat it out. I wouldn't have liked it anyway.

Then the lights on the chair flashed and it started. Something buzzed and then talking started in my head.

"Relax . . ." said the voice. *"An investigation, your mind and all your memories. Do not try to remember, we will do all that. Take the Sleep . . . you will not suffer . . ."*

It was a beautiful voice. Deep and tender . . . *oiled*, but rugged enough to reassure you. An honest voice . . . a real voice, but I didn't Sleep, I didn't go out. Maybe it was that I hadn't taken that drink . . . then I recognised the voice. It was the Machine, of course, speaking like when it had promised me a name. Perhaps that was why I liked it so much.

It was persuasive, it nearly worked, but the Sleep didn't come. I half sat there, half lay in the Teacher's chair, beginning to remember things that I'd forgotten.

"Your mother? The circumstance of your birth?"

There was nothing in my head about that. I just got an image of the Boy trying to kill me and that didn't seem relevant. Then the Machine probed again and asked about my father. There was nothing there either, it was just too long ago.

"Further . . . liquid places . . . comfort? Security?" The probing in my head built up to a pricking sensation. Suddenly I was falling down a place like a dark Street. Old things came up; snatches of words, fragments that didn't make any sense but had a clarity about them. A precise quality of detail like when I had a tube, but without ever seeing the *whole*; there were words too, more and more, too many words that I was surprised to know.

The Machine didn't know I was there. I wasn't supposed to be watching as they took my mind down; it was hard, I was in two places, in two worlds. I could see my Teacher reading the reports as they came out of his chair and I watched the Machine as it looked at me.

Once I saw dark, complicated sequences of numbers and I saw Corps men walking amongst them. Then there were shapes of silent instruments all lit violet and confused with flashes of my spinning floss tray. It didn't make sense to me and perhaps the Deep Machine wasn't getting what it wanted because that pricking kept coming back. What I saw stayed disjointed and even then I was thinking of the bloody things they did in the Rites. It's always bad what we do to people's minds . . . minds are what *really* exist.

It kept going deeper and more fragmentary. The dark instruments kept coming back and somehow they were important. Down there there were radiations I had to think about, a parade of Machines, hummings monsters in their dangerous lights. There were Teachers and Corps men in white coats and there was significance in it all for me.

Something . . . something, it was long ago, or long *behind* something, around corners of my thoughts that I couldn't quite turn. There was a *treatment*, perhaps a convalescence or decontamination, it was too far away to matter much but it seemed I'd been happier once, that there'd been a Purpose and it meant something.

In the middle of seeing my floss tray again it all stopped. I came back with a jerk and there was the smell of smoke.

My Teacher sat facing me and looking puzzled. Behind him there were Teachers and boys running everywhere, girls too, their skirts hitched up for speed. Something really bad had happened. The music had stopped.

My Teacher frowned for a moment, then his face dissolved into fear. His eyes went wild and the wheels on his chair churned turf and he drove back and away. Everyone was wheeling all ways and I was forgotten.

I slowly pulled myself together. It was hell coming back like that from where I'd been. Everybody was running, angry boys hurried out of the tents and domes, the Teachers screwed themselves in tight circles. Someone had done a little shooting, one of the tents went up burning like a wisp of straw, a couple of the domes had holes in them and one was sagging as the fire in it took hold.

It wasn't so bad for me. Sure, it was a bad moment when there was no music, but it didn't hit me like the rest of them. I'd always liked it low anyway, and when it was gone I found I didn't care too much. Somebody told me once I was tone deaf, maybe that is why I didn't miss the controls when the music went. I just lay and came back to full consciousness. It was no time to get noticed. I looked for Wolf, but he'd gone. I suppose the shooting had frightened him, he never did like explosions.

Then the Boy showed up. He came running through the people with a knife in his hand and I thought he'd cut my throat as I lay there. He put the knife under the straps that held me and cut me free. I got out my gun and made sure the wheels were wound.

"Come on!" said the Boy. "I can't let them have you! I've cut the tapes and we've got to go before they find out!"

"What happened? Tell me what happened!" The Boy threw bright coloured lacy things at me. They were Lady Teacher's clothes.

"You didn't panic!" K shouted over the din. "I *told* them you were different. I *told* him who you are! Put on the clothes! We've got to disguise!" He clapped a padded bosom thing around me, fastened it at the back. "Hurry! They're all mad again! Mad the way they really are without the music!"

When those woman's things touched me I could start to protest. I swore and asked why we just didn't make it back to that Cottage in the mirrors.

"You broke the seal when you went through that window." I didn't know what he meant but he sounded pretty sure. "Anyway, I still can't figure how you found that window, if you're blind, I mean?"

I quickly put on the rest of the filmy things. K wriggled his head through his own disguise and when I turned back he'd painted his face and he made quite an attractive girl. Then he asked me why I'd run from the Cottage.

I looked really hard and he was smiling to himself, but that might have been the look of me in all that lace stuff. I couldn't see how he could have forgotten that he'd tried to kill me.

"Anyway . . . no time now! Come on!" He clapped one of those lead masks over my face—the sort Lady Teachers wore with the thick painted red lips—and hustled me off

70

through the people. "Now you do as you're told or they'll get you. They'll be looking when they get the music started again!"

We made it towards the Street in the girls' Rites where their burning pens were. The place was seething with half naked girls and Lady Teachers all aimlessly running. The Boy didn't even look at them, he was just watching me and laughing. I guess I looked pretty stupid.

"You should see yourself!" he said. "We're supposed to be made in God's image! We're supposed to look good!" I couldn't see anything funny in that either.

We hurried past that main Street because the Boy said there was a quieter one further on. We dragged out across that thick musical sand and only just made it. Right then, just as we got on to the apron there, the music came back and things went quiet behind us.

I looked back and saw my Teacher watching us from a hundred yards back. I saw him throw down a message ribbon and then, without warning his chair swung towards us and he fired all his armament.

The first charges tore up a great cloud of the sand in a blaze of fire and mad sounds.

"God!" screamed the Boy. "They know who you are!" We dived over the Street edge and the next blast crashed into the sky above us. I looked and a great area flickered from blue to black and back again. I saw vaulting up there, and great hanging chunks of concrete. I don't think I was surprised. It was only one more layer of illusions . . . God knows there were always enough of them.

I was really worried now they knew I was Candy Man. I grabbed up my skirts and ran down the dark ramp, trying my hardest to catch the Boy.

CHAPTER EIGHT

FIFTY YARDS DOWN the ramp the Boy opened one of those manholes and we went through. Right inside there a flood or rotten nutrient came running down the Street. We had

71

to go through it and that was bad. Then we started climbing on through the girders and pillars.

It was just exactly the same as before, except this time we stank worse than the place did. I wanted to go up, but the danger was up there and anyway the Boy wanted to go down. He seemed to know the way, he told me where to go and I obeyed.

At first we rushed on as fast as we could. Too fast really, the beams were as slippery as a helterskelter, and there was debris falling past us all the time. The ladders down weren't any better—twice I went climbing and slipping down and then found the ladder had broken and the end was swinging loose and sudden in empty space.

After another near fall we eased up and took our time—it was safer and, anyway, we were further from the Rites and there was no sign of pursuit. We were a thousand feet down by then and we'd been working left, we started talking but then our voices sounded so lonely we stopped.

All the time there were fewer and fewer lights. I thought that maybe there'd been a disaster or something, but the Boy told me that they were never on down there. Even the music was intermittent, nothing was sure in the girders, nothing was clear and safe, nothing was *reasonable*. I wondered why they bothered to invent places like the mirrors or the pinkness. It ought to have been confusing enough between the Streets for anybody. I certainly worried myself with things I thought I saw there, but really, the reality ought to have been bad enough for anyone.

I asked the Boy where we were going and how far it was. He wouldn't say, maybe he couldn't, not exactly. He just said we had to keep on going down until we got to the bottom.

Mind, that was a new idea to me—a *bottom*. That meant that there was an end to the Streets, which was something I hadn't ever thought about. People didn't consider that possibility, not in those days.

When I did think about it the idea seemed reasonable, as if maybe it wasn't such a new idea after all, as if there was something in it that I should remember. It was another of those important things behind me that were dark and that I was worried about. It seemed that there might be something I should have done and hadn't yet, an *uneasiness*. A promise to someone dying maybe, something at the bottom of what was happening to me. I just gave up thinking and did what the Boy told me. It was always easier to do what people told me.

We went down another hundred feet and then, when we were going through a dark patch and I was halfway down a ladder, my feet came on to hard, wet sand.

I had a bad moment as I fell over backwards. A moment of total panic until I landed safe on my back. I lay still and groped very carefully about me. It seemed to go on so maybe it was safe. It was almost dark there . . . you could hardly see at all.

I sat up and looked around to see just what I could see. There were half a dozen lights away to the right and they repeated vertically above each other. It was very cold. There were lights above too, very far away, where we'd come from. Regular patterns that had broken down, radiating away from the Streets and into the girders. It was like looking at some ordered and changed sky, some alien thing that had begun to break up. A very long way away there was a hint of music and under it all I thought I could smell smoke.

Then I saw the Boy standing a yard away from me, looking in the other direction. He was only a dark shape against some distant haze of light, but I could see he was checking something with that toothpick of his.

"Get up. It's safe. There's nowhere else to fall from here." He turned back to me, tucked the toothpick into his false bosom. He put down a hand and helped me up. "This way."

He led off, his skirts scraping across the cold sand. There was nothing to do but to follow him. I started to think how, later, when there was a Speaker, I might still report him. I always needed tubes . . . and they still might give me my name for him. It was the Boy that had burned the Rites. Or I could say so anyway.

We soon came to one of the Street ends. There was a small forest of girders there. Lighter ones, not as thick as the ones between the Streets. They were made like inverted vees, the narrow ends buried deep in the sand, the girders spreading as they went up to meet the dark mass of the Street end five feet above. We started walking through there and I stumbled. My back came up against the Street and it was humming so much that it stung me.

I yelled and that frightened the Boy. He called me a fool and then told me how it was where the Anti-Gravity was working.

Then he explained that it wasn't the wind that carried things up the Streets but the Anti-Gravity engines in their roots. He said the air moved up the Streets because of the engines and that was the wind—and it took care of the ventilation. Then he asked me how I thought they could keep the Streets up there without the engines, he said that these days they weren't all working very well and that some weren't working at all, but I knew that already. It was another of those mysteries that I understood perfectly as soon as someone told me, somehow the answer had always been there underneath my mind.

We walked on through the Street root and eighty paces later we came out. I'd hardly got the crick out of my back when we hit water.

Dark and calm it was. So still you wouldn't know it was there, looking as if it'd never moved. Those lights that were above each other were half reflections, of course. You could have seen a long way down there, you could see some very distant lights because all the Streets seemed to end seven feet above the water and below that there were only the small vee struts. The big girders were far above, built up between the Streets.

"Ah!" said K. "You go back on to the sand and wait for me to call. I won't be long."

I stepped back and stood there having a tube and listening to him splashing. Then, as my perceptions sharpened, I thought about that stinking lace hanging on me and how K was probably washing. The sour nutrient clung in my nostrils and I wondered why I didn't bathe too.

I tore off what was left of the Lady Teacher's clothes, then unclipped my rubbers and peeled them off. I shivered some and put my gun and powder carefully where I could find them again. I took my rubbers under my arm and went into the water about knee deep. I started to get cleaned up and it was so cold it almost hurt me.

I was just screwing up courage to splash water on my shoulders when the big lights high up on the Street flickered once, then came on for five seconds before they went out again.

It was only that little time but it was brilliant. Everything was revealed. A great half circle of shallow water and the pale green sand under it, you could see the clean beach behind us and a bank of white pebbles beyond that.

K yelped and splashed. I turned that way and she wasn't the Boy any more. She was a girl about sixteen and beautiful. Long wet blonde hair all let down and breasts and everything. She turned quickly away, I fell over backwards and the light went out.

I was shaken, embarrassed too. I didn't let anyone see me naked. Especially not women. My skin, it was funny. Dead white and very smooth from being under the rubbers. I didn't have body hair either and I didn't like people to see that. I didn't like to touch them either, or them touching me, it was why I wore the rubbers and my gloves—but I said that before. I didn't like to touch myself either.

Anyway, I yelped too and splashed back into the water. There was a deeper place there and I went right in over my head. The water was salt.

Then the light came on for good and the music started really loud from the Speaker near it. I had other things I was thinking about then. I mean, that light and the Speaker could only mean that they were starting to find us. Maybe they could see and hear us too, maybe they knew where we were already, maybe they'd turned on the light because they knew exactly where we were. I was shivering again and I was really worried.

The Girl, that K, she was laughing and holding a white cloth thing across her front. I couldn't see anything to laugh at. She splashed across shaking the water out of her hair and laughing at me sitting in that icy water with my naked, hairless white knees up in front of me, stupidity written all across my face.

"You . . . you're *funny!*" Hell, I had a right to be. I'd

75

just nearly drowned. "I'm not so bad, surely?" Girls . . .
they only really care what they look like.

"You're very nice," I heard myself saying. "But the
light . . . that light . . . the *Speaker*! They can see us!"

She stopped laughing. Then she looked hard at me.

"You admit you can see! That's something—never mind
the lights—they'll take hours to get here." Then she laughed
again. "Your *face*!" She came across the water and ruffled
my hair into my eyes. Then, still laughing, she splashed to
the beach where her pack was. "Come on, Candy! You
said it, we can't stay here!"

She got fresh clothes out of her pack. By the time I'd
finished washing my rubbers she was dressed and ready.
She had on a sort of kilt thing this time. Made of leather
it seemed to be, reaching almost to her knee boots, but I
saw later it was made of the same stuff as my rubbers.
Now she'd got rid of those baggy knee breeches I wondered why I'd ever thought she was a boy—she wasn't
very tall and now she'd let her long hair out from under
the short wig she'd had before, and the whole thing
seemed ridiculous. She smiled when she looked at me
putting on my rubbers.

"It's like you, Candy, like your skin. What's the difference?"

"What's wrong with wearing rubbers? Your people
have them too, I saw them. I got mine out of a box in
some rubble . . ." I'd had a set before that too, I remembered that then. I couldn't think where they'd come from,
so I didn't mention it. K nodded and looked thoughtful,
but she didn't say any more. I finished checking my gun
and we went along the dark shore.

All the time we were moving in that narrow dangerous
space under the Streets. When the place wasn't humming
with the Anti-Gravity they were moaning with the weight
above. Some of the vee structures were bent and buckled,
all around them littered with shards and fragments that
had fallen off above.

It was a chilling place down there, so *still*, so silent except for the varied humming and noses from the Streets.
It was the roots down there, the roots of everything. A
primeval place, *deep*, rock bottom, the roots of the world.

The Girl produced a small light from somewhere but it wasn't strong enough to be much help. We still fell over things half hidden in the sand, washed there I suppose, or maybe revealed by erosion. I wondered where exactly that word 'erosion' came from, it was another of the ones I kept remembering. We found an old rusty thing five feet long, intricate and angular, the corners rounded and heavily rusted. K said it was a gun, or what was left of one. It seemed they'd had their troubles down there too.

Later there were bigger things. Big rusted structures, pressed like troughs into the sand. Paper thin now, hollow and divided up inside, half full of sand, behind and in front there were other rust patterns, pressed into the beach. The Girl said that they'd been tanks once. I remembered them too, or pictures of them, some ancient sort of moving fortress with rockets that fired. I found a skull there, bleached white and worn smooth where the bullet had burst through and broken it.

All the way the lights and music were coming on behind us. They followed all the time, flashing on where we'd been a half hour before. We were gaining, but they were after us now and I didn't like it. The water glinted back there, all under those terrible lights.

Then the Girl looked at her toothpick again, grunted to herself and soon after we struck away from the water. Fifty yards in there we came off the sand and had to climb some rocks before we hit smooth, hard earth. It was higher up there and the Street bottoms were set in holes in the ground, they looked as if they were sinking in. There were some trees up there too, in one place. They were very old, white in K's light, with all the bark fallen off and the smaller branches littering the ground underneath. There were only five trees and right behind them were some great flat cliffs that K called 'buildings'.

Then the lights went on back over the sand and I could see the water all shining around the pillars and catching the white trees against the shadows. We headed more quickly towards the buildings.

"God!" said the Girl. "We lived here once . . . it was the surface. You wouldn't think it now. That's the sea down there, the Atlantic, I believe."

77

"That water . . . ? The sea . . . the Salt Sea?" I'd heard of the Salt Sea. It was an old idea, an ancient thing. I don't know where I heard of it, it was one of those things people remembered, like the Great Robot, or the Saver.

I looked back to get another glimpse of the fabled Salt Sea where it was all supposed to have started. Life, I mean, we were all supposed to have come from there, the mother Salt Sea. I don't know if I believed it, but that's what they said. We'd gone on further and I couldn't see it again, not through the trees, not for the Streets and the structures in between.

K came back and pulled me up the hillside and into the narrow spaces between the buildings and girders—we were well above the Street bottoms by then. There weren't any more trees, but there were a lot of smaller plants there, they just powdered away as we walked through them. The thicker sticks popped as they broke and white dust powdered up.

The buildings were enormous. The Girl's light wouldn't reach their tops or anywhere near it. Where there were girders they came through holes that had been cut in the buildings and big areas had been demolished to make way for the Streets. The edges weren't broken, they'd been cut with heat and always in perfect circles. It was all like that cheese they used to make with holes in it. One place we found a hole that had been blocked off with lumps of stone and mud. There were some brittle strands of long dried grass on the mud and inside were some pots and a broken table.

"Some preferred to take their chances down here," said the Girl. "The Teachers really tried, but they could never make everyone do exactly the same thing."

There were square silvered windows along the bottom of the buildings. The Girl was checking on her toothpick all the way along. When we got to where she wanted she had me kick a window in and we went through.

It was funny inside. The room looked much bigger than it really was for a start. It was made that way, painted too, you crossed it in four paces and it looked twice as wide.

"All they really cared about was space," said the Girl.

"Real or not, it didn't matter so long as they thought they had it . . . so long as they could fool themselves."

Every room we went through had a screen. Pictures still moved in some of them, but nothing that would make you stop to look. Every room had a window too, they were all silvered, so that you couldn't see out even if they were in an outside wall.

"It's high here," said K. "The water never reached, not quite. Some lower compartments are still filled with mud . . . mud and sand." The rooms were pretty and tidy and they looked as if they'd been well cared for once. It's funny, the things that the people had kept. Hoarded and treasured as they lived behind their blind, silvered windows. Once in a while K would stop, pick something up, look at it and perhaps slip it into her pack.

The windows puzzled me for a while, but then we came to some rooms where they were still switched on. They were some sort of screen that carried projections of vast distances, they really opened the rooms out. It was almost like being in the mirrors again. I was uneasy, walking past those hundreds of repeating vistas, room after room.

Mostly they were mountains and lakes, a stand of twelve pines on a spit sticking out into the foreground water. Great piled clouds tumbled up behind the mountains and the colours were garish. They were all the same except sometimes they showed different times of the day or year. Like you'd see a dozen blood red sunsets and then you'd walk past one where you saw the place under ten feet of snow at night with a million cold stars above. Once in a while there'd be a different one, a moonlit desert, or an aerial view and that'd really be a shock.

"Snow . . ." said the Girl, as we passed that one. "None of them would have ever seen that. They wouldn't have seen stars either . . ." I wondered what was bothering her, they were long gone from that place and they were right. You couldn't blame them, it was the sort of place that could drive you mad.

After a while she stopped at one of the Streets where it came punching up through the floors. There was a white cross daubed on there and a white ladder, fresh and new, led up into the darkness.

79

"Up here." She jumped out across the dark space and landed clutching on the ladder. "Come on!" She went up a few rungs and held her light so that I could almost see. I was worried again, worried at all that darkness stretching away down there, but I made it anyway and we started to climb.

We climbed up there until we reached the top, but we couldn't see any more from up there, it was as dark as ever. The Street went on up into the darkness, but the ladder stopped. We made awkward jumps off on to the top of the buildings and lay there gasping. After a while I found a pebble, crawled back to the circular, burned edge and dropped it off into the darkness.

We lay there and waited, listening to the moaning of the Street.

When I'd given up waiting and was feeling about for another pebble, a tiny splash came echoing up from infinity below.

"The sea," said the Girl. "That beach we were on, only a small place, an island. The buildings are out over the seas too . . . we're on their roof now." As if that splash was a signal lights came on down there and the music started too. We didn't wait to look.

The Girl led away across a flat, tarred surface. Almost at once we came on to hard earth and there were small holes to trip you up that K said had been ornamental ponds. There was nothing living up there at all, once we went through some more dead trees and I kept falling over the tarred paths. It might have been paradise gardens once, but it wasn't any more.

A mile on there was a low hill. We sat on a rock and I heard K talking into her toothpick again. A light winked on in the valley in front. I got up to run but the Girl stopped me and we started down towards it.

When we arrived it was another of the Cottages. The door opened for us and we went in. When the lights went on we found we were holding hands and I didn't want to let go. We kept on doing that and smiling at each other. Really I found I didn't mind touching her, in fact it was all right. I mean, she was OK, really she was beautiful, perfect and clean. All the best went into the Corps, I hadn't seen any proper women I'd liked except her, you couldn't compare K with those other ones on the Streets, any way, at times she'd seemed to like me.

Then, at last, she let go and told me to close the door. I took one last look out into that unpleasant, cold darkness, at those dangerous lights shining up the Streets and over the hills and I shut it all out. There was a big key inside so I turned it. I came back into the warmth of the Cottage, to the light and to K.

There was a row of pots in the back, dark brown and turning lighter as they dried ready for firing. There were a couple of boxes under the table, the last of the pots were in them and they were all broken.

The Girl had gone to the wall and rolled it back, she was waving her toothpick about and checking the lights. Then she turned and looked at me. Up and down, very slowly, as if she was thinking about me. Then she held out her hands and I went to her.

"I'll take you to a place," she said. "I know a place . . ." There was that dimming of the Cottage as the power acted. Then the lights went out and there was sunlight streaming in at the windows. The Girl smiled and put up her face for me to kiss, so I kissed it.

CHAPTER NINE

WE MADE LOVE and then she took me back through the door we'd come in at. It was in some other wall now, of course, or at least the outside was—but I was used to that idea by then.

We stepped out into the sunlight and I saw butterflies dipping and bobbing over a sea of flowers. There were elm trees beyond at the bottom of a long garden. You could see that river I saw before shining white through the trunks. Those elms, there wasn't a bit of lichen on any of them—and the butterflies were only two inches across.

"Cabbage whites," said the Girl. "They'll ruin the whole

patch . . ." Then she said that she'd forgotten to close the consoles and went back into the house.

I went off down the garden paths. I was in a daze. The Girl . . . that K . . . *her* for a start. You had it where it was offered on the Streets, I always had my chances; and if I was told, I took them. This time it was different. When K called me I'd discovered a tenderness for her, a feeling like I wanted to protect her. But it couldn't have been that exactly, she never even looked as if she might need that! Not when she was killing all those Teachers. Then there was the way she seemed to be changing all the time. I thought how she was so *young*, I kept telling myself that they always said how like love hate is.

Then there was the garden and the Cottage. I'd never seen anything like it. It was so *good*. It felt so right, so relaxed in the soft air and singing insects. I could hardly believe it. It was like wonderland, like good things could happen there.

I picked a flower and that smelled good too. I tore it to bits and it still felt real. It was all tremendous, it was amazing, it didn't feel in the same universe as the Streets. I started wondering what a man like me had to do with a place like that, why it was and why I was there. I was confused, I'd seen so much in the last few days and it was hard to keep track of it all.

On the right, over against an old red stone wall, was a tree covered with white flowers. An elaborate cast-iron seat was in the shade there. I turned towards it to have a sit, to think maybe, to have a tube. Perhaps that flowery tree looked too good to be true, perhaps I wanted to touch it a little. I went down the grassy paths, brushed through the lavender, passed by the sunflowers.

As I got near, one of the branches jerked down then flew up again. I looked and a woman in a white hat and dress came round the tree. She had an armful of flowers and one or two plants that she'd uprooted. There were petals from the tree on her shoulders.

She saw me and her jaw dropped and she blushed like fire. I felt for my gun, but I'd left it in the house.

"I . . . I thought it was empty . . ." She waved the flowers towards the Cottage. "I did not think that you would mind . . ." Or that was the sense of what she said. She had a funny way of talking and it was hard to understand her at first. I didn't say anything.

A man came then and looked embarrassed too. He had a striped jacket thing on, tight white trousers and polished brown shoes.

"Good afternoon . . ." He looked hard at my rubbers then back up to my face again. "Uh . . . only a few flowers. It . . . well . . . it looked *empty*, do you see?" He was really puzzled by my rubbers. He didn't know what to make of them at all.

"Now, look, old man. You ought to say . . . creeping about dressed like that . . ." He started to get angry, then curiosity got the better of him. "What *is* it that you are wearing?"

"A diving suit," said the Girl from just behind me. "A new sort of diving suit. My husband is an inventor." I hadn't heard her coming but I was glad she was there. She spoke the language well. I guessed 'husband' meant me, but I didn't know what an 'inventor' was. "Please help yourselves to the magnolias," K went on. "They *are* lovely."

"Yes . . . thank you," said the woman. She was looking embarrassed again and the man had taken off his hat. "Thank you . . . we thought the house . . ."

"Not at all," said K. "Take as many as you like. There are camellias over there . . . they are almost out." She went across and got some of the other flowers for the woman.

The man talked to me about my 'diving suit'. I hardly understood him so I just grunted. He kept on smiling and talking, pretending he didn't expect any answers.

They went quite soon. Loaded down with flowers, talking happily to K and throwing sideways glances at me. At the gate the man raised his hat again and waved to me as they went out. They were nice people and they didn't have a weapon between them.

K turned and smiled. She called me to her and I went. We had a good time while we stayed in that Cottage. We boated and fished on the river, or on the pleasant sea just around the point. I used to collect milk for K from the farm up the lane. As rich as custard that milk was, still warm from the honey coloured cows. I still remember how K enjoyed it.

The people were good too. They used to come to talk to K in the evenings, bring presents of strawberries, or fish, or perhaps a couple of pigeons. I'd catch them staring at me sometimes, they used to come partly to look at my rubbers. K'd talk about 'experiments' then, and 'The Admiralty' and it would be all right. She told people that I had to wear the suit for a long time to see what happened and they'd look knowing and nod their heads. They were pretty nice, very kind and their children were always fat. Once I saw a man with a gun, but he was shooting rabbits with it.

It was so quiet there that after a week I was down to one tube a day, but then, it was soft and I wasn't doing much. I hardly thought of the Streets. I'll always remember that time.

I asked the Girl once what the Corps would say to her taking time off like that, but she laughed and said they wouldn't miss her, that she had leave to come anyway. Then we went down through the moonlight to swim in the river.

There were other clouds though. It was the doing nothing that was wrong. I felt useless. You can't be making love all the time, and that was all we did together really, that was what was important to the Girl, the central thing about our relationship. I was afraid it might be the only thing, I mean, I needed more than that. When I wasn't talking to K I wondered what I should be doing, sometimes I'd spend all night twisting and turning about it. It got so bad sometimes that if there'd been a Speaker there I believe I'd have reported us just to ease my mind. I used to jump up screaming and shouting that I'd done it and they'd given me my name. It was the Purposelessness that got me, the *wondering*, that old worry about *why*.

Then, one sunny afternoon when we were sitting on that iron seat under the magnolia, it got solved for us both. That cat came.

That one with the steel claws from the first Cottage. I

looked up and it was standing in some hollyhocks, one paw up, looking out at us.

I got up quickly and yelled. The cat twitched its tail, crossed its eyes and ran, twisting and bounding, back towards the Cottage.

The Girl stood up. Her tea cup splashed down and broke. She tore her blouse open and snatched her tooth-pick from in there.

It was too late. The cat was already through the door even as it closed. I got there about then but I heard the lock click home even as my hand got to the latch. K ran up and waved her toothpick but it was too late.

We stood and looked at each other. K slowly buttoned her blouse. She'd lost a cameo brooch she'd worn since we'd come there and she had to hold her collar together. Then she ruffled my hair the way she'd done down by the dark Salt Sea.

"Say goodbye," she said, close to my ear. "They won't let you get away with this." She moved back, looked at me steadily. It almost felt playful the way she kissed my cheek. "Everything ends . . ."

I put my arms round her and we stood there looking at the door and waiting. The Cottage had suddenly become a threatening, an alien place. We might never have lived there together.

It was only three minutes. Then the door flung open with a crash and somebody in blue knee breeches and a loose silk blouse came bursting out. It was the Boy again.

The Boy! I clutched K in then held her off and looked at her face, then quickly back to the Boy again. They were the same, their faces were identical, they were identical twins. Just her face was a little softer, that was all. You couldn't have told them if they were apart.

But it *was* him! I couldn't think about it. That same baggy blouse, those shapeless velvet knee breeches. That same ugly pistol too.

I felt K's arm tremble but she surely wasn't as worried as me. Then the Boy turned and saw us. He pulled back his upper lip to show his teeth and started waving his pistol towards us.

"You really can't live now, Candy," he said. "You really can't have her and expect to live . . ."

"Nothing to do with you!" said K. I was just watching the pistol. They shouldn't give weapons like that to kids like him.

"Move away from him, sis . . ." I wished I had Wolf. I wished I had my dog. I realised I hadn't missed him all that time since the Rites. I just couldn't think of anything to do. I stood there wishing I had Wolf. I'd have sent him then jumped myself.

"No! I won't do that! It's not his fault!" K was still smiling. I thought maybe she didn't realise the Boy wasn't playing.

"You . . . you're in enough trouble now. You can't do what you did, not with one of them. He's off the Streets. Practically an Alien! Hardly human . . . dirty . . ." I began to move very carefully and slowly towards where there was a flower pot standing on an iron table.

"You meet someone you want to kill him!" K was still smiling, but it was a tight little grin now. "Anyway, Candy's probably . . ."

"You meet someone you want to lay him!" K stepped forward and slapped the Boy's face.

"It's love . . ."

"You'll get over it!" The Boy grinned at her. He rubbed the red mark where she'd slapped him. I could see that scar there from where I'd shot him all of a week before. It was almost gone . . . there was only the whiter line across where he'd been slapped.

"I do what I like. I do it with who I like!"

"Sis, think what you're doing. We're in the *Corps* . . . it's our family. You can't collect men like artifacts. You can't throw away the Corps . . . they'll put you on Earth with the Teachers!" They'd forgotten me for a moment. I made it to the flower pot. It was heavy, full of soil.

"I'm in trouble myself," went on the Boy. "Just being your pair . . . and you going about in my clothes. Doing those things. Look, sis, understand me. I'll burn you both if it'll save me . . ." He was smiling now. I suddenly saw how much he was enjoying himself. He licked his lips. "I'll burn you both down! OK then. Anyway," he jerked his pistol at me, "he cut me twice, whatever happens he's got to die."

He brought his hand up to touch his cheek again. Maybe he was wearing cosmetics, maybe they partly hid the scar, but it had sure healed quickly. Right then I got the table and threw it at him. He went down under it and the flower pot took him in the forehead. He landed on his back in a shower of earth and broken earthenware.

The Girl screamed. The Boy started up spitting blood and teeth. He reached for the pistol and I went for him as fast as I could.

The cat jumped out of the door at my head but I saw it coming and ducked. It twisted, all steel teeth and flashing claws, it turned in the air to get me. I chopped it down with the side of my hand and it smashed against the wall. There was plenty of time.

The Boy was still reaching for his gun. He looked up and saw me coming. He opened his mouth to speak, his hand closed on the pistol, so I stepped on it. I reached for his neck to put him out. Suddenly I knew just how to do that.

"No!" The Girl tugged at my arm. Maybe she thought I was going to break his neck. Hell, I'd sure had enough of that Boy right then, but I wasn't going to do that. I couldn't really *kill* him, not with my bare hands, anyway he was K's brother after all. While she was helping him up I got to the pistol and slipped it inside my rubbers.

Then we stood for a few seconds looking at each other. The cat was fizzing quietly at the bottom of the wall. I didn't mind about killing the cat, even if it was intelligent, it was still only a robot. Then the door opened again and that distinguished looking Fat Man the cat belonged to came out.

"Ah . . . a pleasant world . . ." He was quite calm. He looked down at the jerking cat. "Take it for repair, will you?" The Boy frowned, opened his mouth to protest, then nodded. He stopped sucking his fingers where I'd trodden on them, picked the cat up by its tail and carried it into the Cottage. I saw it twist up and claw him and that made me feel better.

"You're so quick," K told me. "So quick . . . dangerous . . ." I didn't say anything. I could be like that at times, when there was a special danger. I think it was the tubes. I was watching the Fat Man, but when I glanced at the Girl she was smiling.

"Well," the Fat Man said at last. "So we've found you. It took a while. I hear you've been burning down the Teachers?" That was it, that was why I was worried, I'd hated the Girl killing them like that. The Man was serious, he wasn't smiling at all. "I hear you've been disturbing the Rites too." The Girl lowered her head.

"Surely I needn't remind you? Surely you must know how careful you have to be about . . . about fraternisation with the natives? That they are in a decadent state and we cannot afford to mix with them. What you see in *that* I don't know!" He jerked his thumb at me as he spoke.

"I think he might be important," said the Girl. She emphasised the word 'important' and the Fat Man's eyes flicked at me. "But I heard him singing—preaching, they call it—and I don't know. He's *different* from what we expected. Trying to change things on the Streets. Under the power of the Teachers, it didn't seem *right*."

"I know all that. You told us. That's why I sent your brother to check him . . . and on *you*! I know what you can be like!" The Fat Man paused for a moment, he seemed to be getting angrier. "And all that Boy could do was fight Teachers! Fight this fellow! You're nothing but trouble—both of you!"

"He was worth it," said the Girl. "Anyway, I had to. He was different and it was my job to find out why, all about things like that. You told me to watch him, to get close to him."

"You didn't have to . . . to *do* it with him!" He spoke with distaste, as though he could hardly bring himself to form the words. They'd both forgotten me. The Girl was smiling a little half smile to herself, like she was thinking how good it had been. I haven't had many, but I never had a woman like her.

"It's *perverted*!" the Fat Man was nearly shouting. "You going with him!" K laughed outright.

"He's not like the rest down there."

"He's dirty, only half a man. You know it's forbidden to have *any* relations with the originals . . . !"

"We're the same. We're all human."

"Sex! Your tastes . . . you'd do anything for something different!"

"He's strong," said K. She knew she was making him angry, but she still went on. "Treacherous—but they made him like that—he can look after himself. Not like those queens in the Corps!"

"Originals are animals!"

"So are we all."

"Speak for yourself! I hope we've some little flicker left . . ." He paused, got a grip on himself. I suspected he was enjoying himself really. "Love! You'll be talking about love next! That damned anthropology of yours! Those old books you stuff your head with!"

"He's worth something for himself!" said the Girl. "He was happy here. I was too, as happy as I've ever been!" They were both getting angry by then. I still thought the Man was enjoying himself, but he really blew after she said that.

"You just wanted it beastly! A bull in a sty! That's what you wanted!"

I thought she'd hit him like she hit the Boy, but she just clenched her fists and looked down. Her ears were very red and she had a tight little grin on her face. Maybe that grin was a smile I thought, maybe what the Man said was true.

"All that time you spent hanging about the Rites! It's destroyed you! You can't tell the difference between them and us!" The Girl seemed to be struggling to keep her face straight. "You of all people, you should know better things!"

Then K was crying. She wasn't the same for two minutes at a time. Somehow all this was a big emotional thing for them and they were enjoying it too. It was like a game between them.

I shifted my feet. I didn't know where I was or what I should do. Somehow there were things going on that I didn't understand. I mean, in the Streets, if some girl or woman asked you, you did it and that was that. Not many did, of course, what with the conditioning they got at the

Rites and the stuff the Teachers put in the nutrient, but when it happened it was no trouble. It never bothered me before unless I was preaching. But K, I liked being with her, looking after her, I didn't want to see her go. I didn't want her taken from me. It was a sort of Purpose looking after her . . . a reason for being.

"Hell," said the Girl. "It's only sex. Can't I keep him for a while?"

If there'd been a Speaker I'd have reported them all and got the hell out. Who'd think a simple thing like that would cause all that trouble? I'd never known I could feel that about anybody. Then she started crying again.

"Oh . . . daddy . . . !" That really shook me. I mean, fancy knowing your father! I hadn't thought of them like that.

"All right," said the Fat Man. He hesitated, weakened. "This trouble . . . we'll keep it to ourselves. I'll try and stop it going any further, stop it being a Corps matter. You'll have to drop him . . . stop that thing!" He jerked his head at me. "When you've finished with him we'll have your brother put a charge through him and bury him in the garden somewhere." The Girl sobbed once and thanked him. Then she stood back and wiped her eyes.

This thing had gone far enough. I started putting my hand inside my rubbers and groped for the butt of the Boy's pistol.

"No," said the Girl. She came back smiling at me and put her arm through mine. She hung on me there, I couldn't have got out the pistol if I'd really wanted to. "I'll want him for ever. He'll never kill him! We'll live here for ever." She was all smiles now that she'd got her way. The tears had stopped like a tap.

"Yes, dear." The Fat Man smiled too. He didn't think it'd be long before they had me under the flower beds. I had the same thought myself. One thing I was sure of, that Boy wouldn't do it. He'd tried often enough and not managed it. Next time I saw him I'd decided to give him a charge to chew on and not to argue . . . I don't know if I'd really have done that.

The Man smiled at us some more and went back into the Cottage. I saw the Boy in there with the cat. He must have been listening because he asked the Fat Man if he was going to let me get away with it. When his father nodded the Boy looked puzzled at first, then very angry.

"I'll bury you!" he yelled at me. "I'll bury you, Candy Man! I'll come back and get you!"

The Man silenced him with a gesture and closed the door of the Cottage. Then they were gone and I was wondering if they'd really let us be.

The Girl came to me and put her arms round my neck. I felt her softness press against me but it wasn't the same as the last time.

CHAPTER TEN

FOR SOME TIME then nothing happened. It went on just exactly like before, us living out our life together in that paradise Cottage. Sometimes I caught the Girl looking at me with a sort of bright-eyed expectancy about her. Then she'd flick her eyes away and I'd be left wondering what it was I thought I'd seen in them. Our loving got more violent too, partly because we stood to lose each other I suppose, but there was more in it than that, it was as if she enjoyed the danger, as if it stimulated her. It was as if she loved me more because it was forbidden.

Anyway the threat was always hanging over us and on our minds. It worried me anyway, even if we never talked about it. That Fat Man might be content to wait for a while, but I didn't think the Boy would leave it for long.

Then little things started to happen. The potatoes got some disease or other and rotted. The stench was terrible everywhere you went, not that we ever went far, the Girl told me not to. The cows in the farm got bloat, I kept meeting that cat too, it was watching us all the time. Then what milk there was always went sour and the Cottage was suddenly infested with rats and spiders like in the lichen woods. After that there were mosquitos and we couldn't even go down to the river, so we had to sit in the potato

91

stink of the garden, or I did. The Girl took to disappearing more and more often. She'd be gone in the Cottage for hours on end, I'd get sick with worry and then she'd be back in the garden or laughing at me out of the kitchen window. I didn't have a toothpick so I couldn't follow her, she would never tell me where she went.

Then one last night we smeared her with something to keep off the insects and went down by the river. She had me sing for her again. I didn't like it much, even then. It didn't seem right to preach for someone who didn't know our miseries, not for her to like it the way she did. I mean, she was all right, she was in the Corps.

Anyway, she enjoyed it in the way she always did, I never saw her more excited than she was that last time. The next day the boy lost his patience and the War broke out.

They came and conscripted me that afternoon. They were tough. Two big men in red caps and with Alsatians tried to grab me over the gate. I threw them off easy enough and then I tried to make it back to the Cottage but there were four more waiting for me there. They knocked me down and sat on me until the other two came up with handcuffs.

It seemed to me that they were a bit rough. They kept on kicking me. They didn't take me back down the path at all, but up it to the Cottage. The boy was there in khaki with leather belts and shoulder pips. He had a riding crop with him and he used it on me as they shoved me through the door. I started to fight but he put a heavy looking pistol on me. One of the men called it a revolver and I didn't know what it could do, so I stood still.

"What about it?" said the Boy. "Is it worth it? Is she worth what I'm going to do to you?" When I didn't say anything he hit me again with his riding crop. "You won't think it's worth anything when I've finished with you—and remember I'm going to kill you one day!"

There was another of those doors across the Cottage. It hadn't been there before and I didn't like the look of it. They trundled me that way and one of the men held it open. The Boy used his foot and shoved me through.

"It's another sort of Rites!" he shouted. "Get in there!"

He laughed and it sounded like the Girl. I had time to wonder where she'd got to, but then the door shut and I had other things to think about.

All the time I knew what was happening was an illusion, it was just too bad to be anything else. There was a lot of screaming and shouting, a lot of other men dressed in khaki. There was no music, but somehow the atmosphere was charged with a vicious quality of total violence. At first it was about being taught to kill people, to kill them first and then hate them because of what you'd done. Perhaps what was wrong was that there was no music . . . perhaps the men needed those controls.

What I remember most are the heavy, nailed boots we all wore, how they echoed up the concrete paths that were all roofed and walled with corrugated iron to make the sound worse. I suppose I was good at the games we played—I was always first up those nets—but it was the *shouting* I couldn't stand, I got confused, sometimes I forgot it was all false.

Once there was something called bayonet practise. A bayonet was a little sword fitted to the end of your rifle. You had to go screaming and charging down a cinder path and stick your bayonet into a straw stuffed sack at the end of it. I'd just got mine in and the sack turned into K. All naked and trussed, hung there like a chicken. It was cold, it was so *real*. I even saw the goose pimples on her. I mean, it seemed so real.

When I fell down she turned into the sack again and the straw hanging out of it. I thought some blood splashed on my hand, but it was only mud.

There was a corporal there leaning over me and laughing. He called me obscene kinds of fool and turned into the Boy. Everybody thought it was pretty funny and while they were laughing the Boy asked me if I'd give up and tell K I didn't want her any more. I told him how I knew it must all be a dream and that I didn't care what he invented to torture me.

"You wait and see about that!" He still sounded just like K. "We've only started!"

Then there was a sea voyage in a dirty, over-crowded ship. I felt terrible. 'Mal de mer' they called it as they laughed at me some more. I was in a long steamy cabin full of men in dark green overcoats who were all being sick too. It was a vision of a sort of hell, all stink and bad breath and coughing. I knew I could take it, I knew it was all a vision but it still hurt. Especially when the Girl came to me at night and nobody else saw her. I suppose they let her do that for contrast, it certainly made me cry in the mornings when she went.

I have a memory from a little later of going down a swaying gang plank and people cheering us. The Boy was in the crowd, waving a flag and shouting with the rest of them. He kept coming and trying to get me to deny K. I still thought I could take it, but when we'd marched up to the fighting I wasn't so sure. That Boy was pretty sick to have dreamed up the things men did there . . . the weapons they had. The flame throwers and the war gas—it was so hard to remember it was an illusion.

There were a lot of men killed. Nothing came near me except once when a sniper found me and his bullet chopped a lump out of my rubbers. There was a long time when I was running from him under the barbed wire and machine-gun bullets. I could tell the sniper was the Boy from the way he kept missing me, but I ran all the same.

"Only softening up!" I heard him yell at me. "There's more yet!" It got that it was a relief when he taunted me. I knew then it wasn't happening and all I had to worry about were my cold, wet feet and the lice.

Once I hid in a dug-out that was full of dead men. It was bad but I lay still and didn't mind too much until they all turned into K; all dead a long time of various things. I remember a gas attack too. The man next to me was suddenly choking like a maniac inside his faulty gas mask—and then he became K too. It was so *cruel*, she was so close, but infinity away beyond that wafer of celluloid. It was hell to watch, but really I knew it was just too fantastic to be real, too *bad* and that it hadn't really happened to her.

When I put my hands out to help it changed again and I was the one inside that mask. Then it was agony and everything faded.

For a moment I thought it was all over and the Boy had given up, but then I found myself in a cellar and two men in brown shirts were beating me with hoses.

"Well?" The Boy came in and stood beside me. "I'm giving you a chance again. I don't know why." He swotted a fly with his riding crop. There were a lot of flies and they kept landing on where I'd been beaten. "Well . . . perhaps I do know why. She *is* my sister and *you've* got to send *her* away or she'll be upset. She can be just as angry as me—you've got to send her away so I can kill you." He looked down at me for a while. "She's going through this as well, you know. She's watching it— what do you think it's doing to her?" He twisted his fingers into my hair, then jerked my head so that I had to look into his face. "She might even be enjoying it! You think of *that*?"

That scene ended and they were burning people at the stake. I had to whip the Girl, or an image of her, through streets and then I had to put the torch into the sticks heaped at her feet. In a kind of way she was Luckier than me—she had an identity at least. There was a name tattooed right across her front. I had to watch as the clothes with the six pointed yellow star burned off her. She screamed all the time. Honestly, I don't know how the Boy thought those things up.

I went on and on. I remember a narrow battlement with me on it watching men with swords and horned helmets breaking the door down. There were women in there with me and they all got carried off and they were all the Girl. I watched, lying on a smelly rush covered floor with a sword thrust in my stomach. The worst thing was that K looked as if she *was* enjoying it. Like she was acting, throwing out her arms in big gestures.

"Still no?" said the Boy.

"Yes!"

Then it was the cockpit of some sort of aircraft. The Boy was with me and he wasn't sure if the place below was called Guernica or Dresden. We dropped an atomic bomb on it anyway and I could see K down there holding a light out of a window and screaming. I was in trouble not only because I dropped the bomb, which was bad enough, but because I was just far enough from ground zero to survive for a while too.

Then the Boy and I were in a helicopter. He offered me a pistol, butt first. I looked at it and wished it was real, or that I had the powder gun I'd left in the Cottage.

"One charge," he said. "You can kill yourself and end it—save your face that way." I looked at him and he was serious. "She'll always remember you. Otherwise one day she'll just get tired and never think of you again."

"No!"

He put up a foot against me to kick me out of the hatch. I nearly went, but I managed to steady myself and in the struggle I got that pistol and pointed it at him.

I don't know if I really would have killed him. But anyway he disappeared and suddenly K was in his place.

"Please . . ." she said quietly. "Please stop it . . . they're killing you all the time . . ."

"Do you want me to give you up?" I hated to see her break like that. I wondered if it was really her or just an illusion within the dream and sent to fool me.

"Please . . . please shoot yourself?" I still didn't know, maybe she thought it was good advice. They were certainly putting me through it. "Please . . ." she went on. "For me. I'll always remember Candy Man who died for me . . ."

I couldn't do it of course. I couldn't have done it even if she'd made it an order. As I said, the thing I *knew* I *had* to do was to survive.

Her body hit me like a ram. I was off balance. We both sprawled out of the open hatch four thousand feet above a muddy delta. She screamed and I screamed and we went down like stones.

Then suddenly I was lying on a white thing. There were still screams in my ears and my hands didn't stop shaking for hours afterwards. But it was safe, I felt safe in that room, safe and quiet.

The Girl was there. Standing over against the window. The Boy was there too, they were looking at each other and smiling, but not as if there was anything funny.

"K . . ." I called out to her. "Please . . ." Now she was there it was all right again and I loved her like before.

I didn't even want to report anyone for tubes. It was real again now, I knew that . . . anyway, what happened next, that was no dream.

"K . . ." I called out again. Nobody moved. I couldn't move myself. I was fully conscious, but I couldn't move. I was confused too, thinking only of K, everything was a vision of her name. I kept on calling but in the end I wasn't sure I was saying anything for them to hear.

"K . . ." At last she heard. She sighed, unfolded her arms and came across to look down on me. She was dressed like the Boy again. Maybe it was some sort of uniform. She smelled of wood smoke—over on the table was a lamp like I'd seen in my dreams. I looked into her eyes, but they were empty like a mirror. After a moment she went away again.

"How could you do it with *that*?" said the Boy. "Look at him!"

"It was all right . . ." said the Girl. She folded her arms again, then ran her hand up her arms. She looked away out of the window. "It was all right . . ."

"It's disgusting!"

"Isn't it?" She sounded pleased with herself. Maybe I'd won after all. I thought maybe we'd won. "You didn't break him!"

"Hell, no . . . Well, we know now, don't we? Anyway . . . I wasn't allowed to. How could I expect to?"

"I knew all the time . . ."

"Bitch!"

"We had to be sure . . . it was the quickest way. How long will *he* be?"

A door opened and the Fat Man came in. He came straight over and looked at me.

"It's him all right . . . it is him." He turned on the Boy and K. "I told you not to torture him! God . . . if you'd damaged his mind . . . if he'd been killed . . . !"

"Hell! I didn't know!" said the Boy. "How was I supposed to know? Anyway, he thinks it was all illusions —it's only been ten minutes . . ."

"Careful," said the Man. "You can't say where illusions start, where the other thing ends, he wouldn't know that, he's spent his life on the Streets. You might be a dream to him—ever think of that? How do you know what people think of you?" He turned to the Girl. *"You* knew! You knew who he was. I said it before, I'll say it again. You just wanted it beastly . . . any new trick!"

"I had to be sure, as an anthropologist, as a scientist . . ."

"You should have made an official preliminary report! You know how important he is!"

"I told you! I told you I thought he was interesting . . ."

"You're corrupt. Degenerate!" He glowered at her. The Boy sniggered. "The way you wear your brother's clothes, you're just a dirty joke! Transvestite bitch!" He was really angry. I wondered when they'd remember me. I hoped they might let me get up then.

"Necessary," said the Girl dreamily, still half smiling at her brother. "You know what might happen to a young Girl down on the Streets . . ."

"Damn you, no! I know nothing of the sort! They're too dumb for rape, too stupid to want sex. The Teachers stop them wanting . . ." He stopped, then went on more slowly. "You know what they do to people to fail the Rites. You know that wasn't why you . . ."

"Candy used to stir them up . . ." She smiled at some fond memory. "He had a talent for that. He's really treacherous, merciless." She frowned. "Gone *soft* now. Gone soft on me . . ."

"You didn't have to go through the girls' Rites! You didn't have to dress up like that!" It shook the Girl. She swapped a quick glance with the Boy. "Oh, yes! I know! You were too interested in those filthy Rites. I watched you. I sent a cat and watched you through it. You didn't have to hurt those Teachers, just for your thrills! What'll you do when you're tired of everything and nothing excites you?"

I started to protest. He shouldn't talk to K like that, then I thought about it and I wasn't sure any more. Maybe she hadn't gone into the Rites to save me after all. Not that it made any difference what I said, there weren't any sounds coming out of my mouth.

"Setting out with your brother to hunt poor Candy Man like that! Thought it'd be fun to kick him through the Rites? Thought he'd fail? Played him like a mouse! Then fancied him when he saw you naked . . ."

"We . . . I was trying to find out if he was . . . It seemed as if the Rites were a good way to find out quickly."

"Liar. You were playing with him. Like you were torturing him just now, pretending to be each other. You! You're not fit for the Streets!"

They glared at each other. There was a long silence. The Fat Man calmed. He looked anxious and serious; those other two, they just smirked. K . . . it was hell . . . I struggled to get up, to call her name again.

"God . . ." said the Man. "I wouldn't have had you do that to any of the originals. We've got a responsibility. If you've hurt him! Thank God I found out in time, thank God I've found out his name . . ."

I got strength from somewhere. I sat almost up, but I couldn't stay there, I fell back again. There were wires on my head and they held me down.

"K . . ." I got out. I hadn't meant to say that. I'd meant to ask about my name. "K . . ." I sad it again.

She turned then. They all did, but I was looking at her. My arms came up. Her upper lip curled back like the Boy's.

"Dirty Android!" That was what she said. I didn't understand at first.

"Now . . . now *easy*!" said the Fat Man. He yelled at K. "Shut up, you! This is too important . . ."

"Android!" said the Girl. She giggled. *"Dirty,* lovely, loving *Android*! That's you, darling Candy! That's . . ." The Fat Man slapped her hard. The Boy tittered. The Girl sobbed once then went quiet.

"Me?" I sat up, all the way this time. The sheet slipped down. They'd opened my chest and there were wires all over it.

"2/59/9215!" said the Fat Man.

It was my name. I knew it. I listened with a new attention. Nothing was important now except what the Fat Man was going to say. I lay and watched and listened. K wasn't important any more, not right then anyway. Everything was fitting into place, I remembered it all.

CHAPTER ELEVEN

THEY GAVE ME tubes but they didn't let me off that operating slab. When the tubes took effect and I realised that I had my name at last, I knew it would be getting better all the time. I was feeling stronger and stronger, really *Lucky*, as we used to say.

I looked around. The slab was surrounded with bright coloured pipes and coiled wires. A little further away there were tall shining machines all wheeled up and connected to me, then, in turn, fatter cables let into the floor but I didn't care where they went. I saw myself lying there, reflected a thousand times in the bright metal covers. Now that I knew my name and had my Purpose . . . my *Purpose* . . . it didn't seem so bad.

The Fat Man was standing at my feet and looking at me. He held my eyes for a moment and gave me a half smile, but I wasn't worried, for once I wasn't worried. I knew I would soon know my Purpose and I could really take anything. The Boy and K were over across the room somewhere, I saw that we weren't in the Cottage, but some sort of metal place.

Then the Fat Man made a movement towards the consoles on the wall and the blinds came down across the windows and we were plunged into darkness. Strong lights came on, all focused on me. I was left alone in the reflecting brilliance of the instruments and the light-drenched slab. Then I began to see small movements in the warm darkness around me. Sometimes a hand would come into my light island and a toothpick would wink as someone adjusted something, but mostly there were only the voices.

I lay there, relaxed in the brilliance, nursing my revelation, my new content and well-being. It was a lonely place in there, but I didn't mind. I was separated from the Girl for ever and that didn't matter either. Right then

I didn't care what she was or what she did. I was an Android . . . a made man . . . a machine, and if that was true, I was made to do something. I had a reason, I had my *Purpose*. It didn't matter what it was, really it doesn't matter at all; if you've something to live for you can sure go on living. I waited patiently, listening with a kind of cool anticipation, calmly listening for what would come, for what I knew the Fat Man would tell me.

For a long time they discussed possibilities. Once the Girl came and looked down on me, her face dark against the light, her hair a halo of gold. I saw her lip go up and she called me 'Android' as if it was something dirty.

I didn't mind at all. How could she know what it was like? She was human, how could she know what it was like to have a Purpose? Hell, she was from the Corps! She could call me what she liked, it didn't interfere with what I was made to do.

"Don't do that!" said the Fat Man sharply. "You mustn't disturb him now. A delicate time, a subtle thing. They can suffer you know, we must be careful not to ruin him now we've got him . . ." He paused to look at the instruments, his voice tailed off as he got interested in them. I laughed to myself, wondered in my mind why they thought I should care I wasn't human. I was what I was and I had things to do.

"You didn't care so much out at that Cottage . . ." said the Boy out of the honey darkness. He paused. "I think I'll kill him anyway . . ." The Man turned quickly and snarled at him to be quiet.

"After he's . . . after he's done whatever it is we want him for . . ." The Boy went further away across the room. Maybe the Man sent him. The Girl laughed out of the darkness.

I had a moment's startling remembrance of her creamy skin, a vivid instant of regret. It had been all right being a man, some of the time it had been very good. Preaching too . . . singing, I'd liked that . . . and the touch of the Girl, I'd liked touching her. It soon left my mind. It wasn't important at all. What mattered was I had a name.

"Well?" said the Boy. "Come on, tell us what he's good for. Turn him on or whatever you do . . ."

101

Shadows moved through the lights. It was neverland, warm and pleasant. Time had no meaning. An hour could have been for ever.

The Fat Man leaned into the light, shaded a hand across his eyes and looked at a row of small screens. I noticed for the first time that I was strapped down like a monster. I wasn't like that—there was no need. But I soon forgot, it was good lying there in the warmth, savouring my name, waiting to be turned on.

"It's not as easy as that." The Fat Man went back out of the light again. "He's got to do it the hard way, out of his head, out of himself, no one can do it for him."

"Those straps OK?" said the Boy. "He's a big brute!"

"He's a pussy cat," said the Girl. She leaned into the light and I could see her again. She had that cat robot in her arms, its blue eyes stared at me. "He was all right with me." She swayed back, the cat's uncrossed eyes flashed blue at me out of the dark. I was seeing everything, maybe it was the tubes, or maybe they were stimulating me down those wires, pulling at my brain.

"It's not so simple. You can't just turn him on. He's as complicated as a man, it's all in him, what he has to do. What we have to do is reach it . . . remind him . . . reactivate him in that way . . ." The Fat Man was busy at the consoles again. Nobody said anything for a long time.

"Yes . . ." The Boy spoke softly. "I'll kill him later . . ."

"You'll find he won't care then, not when he's finished. Will you want to burn him if he laughs at you, if he doesn't care?"

The Boy went away then. I could hear him out in the dark talking to the Girl. The Fat Man came in close to me. A shining metal stool swung out of the slab. He sat on it, eased quietly in close to me, talking all the time so I would't notice. Then he swivelled on his stool, reached back to the console and did things to it with his toothpick. Maybe he was talking to himself, I couldn't decide.

"Difficult . . . what to give him? As complex as a man . . ." He shaded his eyes in close to those little screens again. I felt that little tingle in my mind like the Teacher had given me at the Rites.

"All that overlay . . ." said the Man to himself. "As if it wasn't hard enough without that, all that *experience*, all that life. Crazy, a thousand years of roaming free, no wonder he's forgotten who he is and what he's for. Crazy to let him roam free!" He looked at me close, his face swam up like a great white moon. He had eyes like a road map, whatever that was. I could smell alcohol on his breath.

"You remember, Candy Man? You remember why they turned you loose?" When I didn't answer he grunted, turned back to those light spangled consoles, waved his toothpick at something there.

The Girl came back into the half light, I saw her put the cat on to the console top. She stood, one hand on her hip, the other ready with her toothpick to make the adjustments the Fat Man signalled. I didn't see how he did that. I saw no movements and I heard no words between them. I tried to stare the cat down, but I couldn't do that either.

"You'll remember!" said the Fat Man. "You'll remember . . ." It sounded like a threat. Maybe he was angry because I'd lived two thousand and seventy years and he was only human.

That warm tingle in my brain redoubled. That same dark Street as in the Rites opened up in front of me and I was falling down it again. I saw my legs kick in the thousand reflections on the instruments. I saw that Teacher's legs too, I remembered them go spinning up.

"All right . . ." said the Fat Man. "All right, it'll be all right. Just sleep like the Teachers told you when they suspected who you might be. Only this time it'll take . . . they didn't know who you were and we do . . . this time it'll tell you your *why* . . ."

I thought how that was a great thing, to know your *why*. I'd been a man so long and now I was going to have a reason, a *why* for my life, for everything that I'd done.

I saw an iceberg fall off a glacier. Then it was gone. I was back in the light again, that warm light and the white moon face of the Man looming over me, the Girl standing there smiling at me out of the gloom. I saw the toothpick move in her busy fingers, then it all disappeared.

I was falling down that Street of memory. The same one like before. Then I was back with the iceberg. I knew exactly what it was. I've never seen an iceberg, except that one. I saw it coming seething and plunging back up out of the sea, the jade water running and swamping off it.

I saw it again and again. I saw the gulls wheeling and the raging of the salt sea around the falling and breaking ice. Then, breaking still, I saw it floating mast high and seven tenths below the surface. I thought how that was maybe some kind of symbol, some sort of analogy out of my mind. God! But the world was like that, seven tenths under, you never knew what to believe. In that instant I remembered.

"That's it!" I shouted. Or maybe I didn't, it sounded like my voice, but I couldn't be sure I was talking. Perhaps it was just thoughts—the Fat Man seemed to understand, and that was what mattered. He leaned back on his stool, then sat very still, listening to all I said.

"The ice melted . . . the ice caps thawed . . . greenhouse effect . . ." I knew what had happened, it was happening again in my head.

"Yes," came the Fat Man's voice. "The ice melted and the seas came up."

I saw visions of the low parts of the World City flooding. I saw dykes built across the corridors and the breaking, rushing water. Terrible, I was right in it, but really it was only something I'd been told. It was like a game, a drama, a tragedy with corpses rising with the water. The Fat Man's voice was always there over it all. That was like a game too, him always there driving me to remember more. Prompting me—and he was only a voice and I was remembering awful things I hadn't remembered before. If I hadn't known I was an Android I might have hated him for it.

Then the visions changed and I saw those Machines again. Those serried *things*. The vast complicated shapes seemed to pulse light down there, that dull brilliant light you couldn't see properly, that feeling, that *ambience* of terrible power.

"Yes . . ." said the Man. He wanted to get on, there was something else coming that was more important to him. "Yes, yes, pumps. Working on the water, they tried to vapourize it off into space, most of it fell back. Get on . . . finish telling me about it."

"No. More than that . . ." I tried to get it, but somehow I couldn't yet. There had to be an order of remembering. I thought it was to do with water, some sense of flowing things, a swirling, a flux, something potent. Those machines, going for ever, making something as well as destroying. Sustaining something? I couldn't think. The Fat Man was impatient by then, he kept telling me to get on. Once or twice he was almost shouting at me, but he seemed to control himself and went on in an ordinary voice.

Then I remembered about the Teachers. The how and why of *them*. How they had a function too.

"Eugenics . . ." I said. "Politics . . . the Rites . . . selection for breeding, the Lady Teacher's Stud . . ." The Girl got interested at that. She came dangling her gold hair into the light, she kept questioning me.

"But it didn't work . . ." she said. "There are as many idiots on the Streets as there ever were. Now *sterilisation*, now that would have really been an answer!"

"They burned their brains when they'd finished with them, and there's that stuff in the nutrient," said the Fat Man. "The Rites were only a filter to get the best genes for the Teachers, and for us, originally."

"Not only that. Originally to benefit . . . to raise the whole race up by selection, to raise it from where it had fallen." I understood it perfectly, I remembered it. Once there had been something called natural selection to take care of the weaklings, to breed out the failure. "Sterilization would have been Anti-Life, we Machines would not permit it."

"They burned brains," said the Fat Man gently. "They made fools of them."

"That had always been permitted."

"But why did the race fail?" It was the Girl that was talking, but the Man was nearer. She peered around his moon face, her hair brushed golden on his armoured shoulder. I began to count the individual strands. "Why the degeneration, why were the Machines necessary in the first place?"

"The Machines," I said. I knew the answer to that one. "The Deep Machines made themselves necessary. It was all too easy for the race with them. A millennium of peace and comfort and all the time the crushing *leisure*. A thousand years of only games to play, of nothing to *do*. The Machines doing everything so much better, a sense of inferiority, degeneration setting in. A vicious circle. Why they made me, why they organised the Teachers, no one else could do my job. When the City began to fail . . ."

I had visions again. Tiered places, many structured, many layered, many peopled. Lights going out, whole continents suddenly dark, sometimes fires breaking. Starvation and hopelessness and screaming riots in the Streets, breaking walls and the Sea still rising.

"Who were the Teachers?" said the Girl. I'd counted seven hundred hairs, they were all different, all beautiful.

"Not Androids. Imperfect men. An hereditary caste. An organisation, rules and precedents, established procedures, as near a machine as a man can be. Designed by the Deep Machines."

"These Machines you speak of . . . the ones with the blue light?" The Fat Man kept coming back to them, maybe he was scared of the big brains. Some men are.

"Partly . . . only partly that." There was something else as well. I fought down after it. Something important, something really *deep*.

"You see!" said the Girl. I'd got to eight hundred and ninety-seven hairs. Some of the shapes had begun to repeat, perhaps she wore a wig. That would have been just like her, perhaps sometimes the Boy dressed as the Girl. "You see!" she went on. "Absolutely traditional! A gerontocracy, self perpetuating! A caste, like a religion! Beautiful! Classic!" She was really excited. It was all she really cared about, she was only really excited by her science. That was all she'd cared about me, that was all she cared about humanity.

"So," said the Fat Man, "we have this picture: the ice caps melting . . . disturbed by the World City, no doubt . . . the water rising, the race grossly over-sized and degenerating . . ."

"There was nothing else to pass the time, the Machines

saw to it that everyone survived to breed again. It was important to the race, procreation was all there was left for them to do, to have *value* in. The thing they could do that the Machines couldn't."

"Birth Control," said the Fat Man. He looked disappointed. "Malthus, all this was long predicted. Surely ..."

"It didn't work, or it worked the wrong way," the Girl broke in. She leaned more into the light, her rings flashed before she spoke. Her hair cascaded down. She was taken up with explaining.

"But don't you see? Statistically the bright ones could do that—remember to take their pills or whatever it was—but the *stupid*! The forgetful—the primitive! Some even thought it was wrong, immoral or something! Think of what it meant down the long generations! Another selection—an unnatural selection for stupidity, for carelessness and irresponsibility!"

"Then that's why the Teachers ..."

"Exactly! That's why the Teachers *existed*!" The Girl was shouting now. "That's what the sect was for! Originally, Teaching birth control in that decaying, overpopulated World City!"

"It failed," I said. "It didn't work ..."

"Too much momentum!" The rings sparkled again. She smiled at me and she really meant it that time. She approved of what I was trying to say. "The trends of a thousand years. Imagine that Babel! Imagine the contradicting arguments, the fighting for ideas, the fighting for *space*! For rights in that degeneration. So they put the power wholly in the Machines! Or the Machines took the power. They had to get it right before it was too late. So they set the Machines to fight the trends and the Machines took the Teachers to help them—to be their agents, probably they were the only organisation left."

"It still failed," I said. I was seeing that hell City. The steamy, stinking packed people, the fear, the decay, the neurotic copulation drive, the frantic assertion of humanity's life. The frantic assertion of being *different* from everybody else. Then blood spilled in the Streets, the barricades and fire bombs, the armed gangs, the way they feared each other, the way they hated.

"Still evidence of that," said the Girl. "Think of those people near the Rites entrance. Think how Candy can't bear to touch . . ."

"And all the time the echo of the sea in the lower levels, the rising sea, the breaking and wearing down there . . ."

"Yes!" said the Girl. "All the time *yes*! That was the way . . ."

I saw the eugenics squads, the Rites and the Teachers with weapons now, frantic religious cults, paranoia, brain burnings, poisons in the nutrient . . .

"WRONG," I said. "A wrong thing to happen, cruel time. Cruel." My voice surprised me.

The Fat Man looked surprised too. He sat back into the shadows, quickly checked the consoles.

"You . . . you're only an Android!" The Boy spoke from somewhere in the darkness. "You aren't allowed to make judgements . . ." He tittered in that nasty way of his. I knew he was right. I shouldn't say things like that. It wasn't my place.

I could see the Man's hands fluttering like birds in the half light as he talked to the Girl.

"I told you he was interesting," she said. "I think I was right to experiment with him. You'd just have sent him down, I still think there's more to know."

"It's only time," said the Fat Man at last. "Only the overlaying of experience. Remember he was made to live amongst people and to pass as one, to seem to be a man."

"Don't send him yet!" There were thirteen hundred and sixty-two hairs that I had counted. They were all almost exactly the same colour and I hadn't seen any that were split. I was sure it was a wig, false, like the rest of her. "Don't send him," she said. "Let me . . ."

"We know what *you* want!" said the Boy. "Perhaps I'll let you have him when I've killed him!" He just didn't understand. We ignored him.

"He's got to go down. It's what he's for." The Fat Man's toothpick waved out over the consoles and I had that brain tingle again. He bent over me. "The rising water. The waves on the stairs, the surf in the lift walls!"

And then I had it. I knew the reason for the world.

"The surface. The surfaces. The World City had mostly

flooded. They built the world again on the roof tops. Covered it all with country and built the City again . . ."

"The time it must have taken," said the Girl. "All the seething people and the water rising and they did that. The society *that* must have been . . ."

"The Machines did it . . . made the first surface . . . they were made to run the new City. It was before my time . . ." I saw the world as it had been. I saw it from space. Marbled land masses across the blue Seas, the land green and brown. I saw the City spread across, pause, then reach out across the seas. I saw the ice begin to go, the clouds thicken, then redouble.

"That's what did it," said the Fat Man. "The trees going, the balance upset, accelerating, out of control."

"But it was only eighty feet in the last stage," said the Girl. "A couple of hundred in all, they had plenty of time . . ."

"Two hundred and three point five mean," I said. "Every three feet displaced nine hundred million people . . ." I saw the new City overlay the old one. I saw collapses, saw them build up again. There were only the mountains left, only the mountains dotted with the palaces of the rich, of the commissars. The Rockies, the Andes, the Alps and Himalayas, smaller places too—and all the time getting smaller as the City raced up against the flooded, smoky hell chaos of overcrowding it spawned in its own depths . . .

"The Machines," I said. "Building up and up the layers, on and on, a closed, vicious circle . . ."

"And one thing more . . ." The Fat Man prompted my memory.

"They couldn't stop them . . ." When the population began to decline, when the Rites had worked and the Machines had built enough, they'd forgotten how to stop them.

"Devolution . . ." said the Girl. "Upset balances, losing, they probably didn't care anyway."

"They *forgot* how!" I said. "But they were automatic, made to stop themselves when they had finished . . ."

"Too long . . ." said the Girl. "Damage maybe. Two thousand years of making the recurring surfaces. And the

Teachers all that time, evidence that they were evolving their function. A sociology, what a *study!*" She was awesome. You couldn't have called her 'whore', not then. She was transcended.

"But still one more thing . . ." said the Fat Man. "One more central fact . . ." I hit it then. It was the biggest thing of all.

"The Matter Engine!" The Fat Man slapped his hands on his knees. He shouted, then started licking his lips. I saw his tongue, a soft pink thing, glistening in the lights. He smiled and sat back.

"They were made to make the surfaces," I said. That's what the deepest of Deep Machines was, bathed down there in their own radiance, down there in its own electric halo of mystery. No wonder they couldn't stop them. No one could stop them but me—and I could only do that because they would help me.

"Yes . . ." said the Fat Man, but he wasn't talking to me. "Matter Engines—the secret of the Cosmos. We had it then . . . stumbled on it. The conditions in which matter creates itself, the coming from nothing to something . . ."

"I am made to stop them." That was it. That was what I was made for . . . that was my Purpose.

"You're the Great Robot . . ." said the Girl. "You're the part of the Machine that's got to end it, end the world. You were made to stop them—you dirty Android."

CHAPTER TWELVE

I WAS GETTING clear pictures right then. All in my head, everything was in my head, I understood it all. Most things anyway, I never felt like that before.

I could see myself going through those old Machines, I could anticipate my path there. Through those difficulties, through those terrible defences. I remembered all the Codes, I could remember it wasn't easy, that there were dangers to face, even for me there were dangers to face.

"You were meant to do it long ago," said the Girl.

"They made you flesh, made you into meat for that." She grinned at me. "Don't get proud, Android. You're just an emergency measure, only a long stop."

"Why hasn't he done it before? He failed too?" You could tell from the Boy's voice he liked that idea.

"Meant to exercise a judgement. When it got too bad for him to tolerate he was meant to stop it." The Fat Man turned and frowned at the Boy. "Careful now, don't antagonise . . ."

"Went wrong too," sneered the Boy. "A failed Android. All he did was sing his songs about it . . . *Preach*!"

"He did that well," said the Girl. "And after . . ." I've noticed that before about women. It's all they care about until they get too old.

"Matter Engines," said the Fat Man. "Think about the Matter Engines. They mean everything."

"He did preach well!" said the Girl. The Man ignored her. He leaned down over me.

"We want a key unit out of a Matter Engine." The Fat Man was appealing to me. Asking for help, a favour of me—an Android. "A 'Toroid' I think it's called, if we could get one of them we could make whole Engines.

"The design is lost, we have records for the rest, but the Toroids are the secret. Those Engines, the ones down there . . . yours . . . they're the only ones we know about . . ." I just looked at him. I started to ask why he wanted them, why they were important to the Corps. The Corps were gods to me. I couldn't see how they could need my help, or the Toroids either.

"We've explored, we've got ships back from the nearer stars, we've gone as far as we can in Sublight. We've got to go on, we've got to be able to go further. If the Corps doesn't go on . . . if the race doesn't go on . . ." He shrugged his shoulders. I knew what he meant. The Corps were the race now. If they didn't go on they'd end up the same way as the men on Earth and the race really would be finished. I nodded.

"We've got to cross the Galaxy . . . go to the Clouds . . . and after that we'll cross Metaspace to the other Galaxies. We *must* go on, we must cross the Abyss. It's go on or die! To go on we must have Translight.

111

"For Lightspeed we need energy. Vast energy! We need the energy of the Matter Engines!"

Those Matter Engines! It was like a conjuring trick. They called the matter out like white rabbits out of a top hat, but really out of nothing. You can't describe it.

"We'll make energy out of the matter. We'll accelerate up. A hundred years of full power! Two hundred . . . a thousand if we need it! We could leave Lightspeed way behind if we have to!"

He was starry eyed. He was a dreamer. He was having a vision and my heart went out to him.

"Why?" I said. "Why should I help you?" My purpose was just to stop the things, not to dismantle them. There was no warrant for it, it wasn't part of what I was made for. I had to have an order, I wanted it, all he had to do was give me an order.

"Twice . . . twenty . . . two hundred times Lightspeed . . . going and coming . . . antimatter . . . new realms, new worlds to conquer . . . time in the palms of our hands. We'll navigate the Rim, cross everything . . ." He really cared about it, he dreamed of success, it was like the Girl and her science. It was what made men great, that *caring*, that *loving*. The bloody minded lengths they'd go to for their loving. I watched him with awe in me. That deep feeling, I respected it, you maybe don't feel things too deeply if you're an Android.

"He won't do it," said the Boy. "Forget it, Fat Man. Shall I burn him now?"

"You must help us," said K. She gave me a smile that was meant to melt me like grease. "It's a *scientific* thing. You must do it!" It was an order. I couldn't refuse.

"All right." The Girl looked pleased when I'd said that. Maybe she thought it was her smile that did the trick.

"And the Probes shall reach out . . ." said the Fat Man. "The stars shall be the road, the Milky Way our foot-path, all across those empty reaches." Dreaming was a fine thing. I loved it, but, God, you could have enough. "Men and Machines . . . the ships and their Riders reaching easy in their indissoluble unity . . . the listening and the reaching, and all the time the Matter Engines living in their lilac light, the patterns of blues, the power and surging of their symmetry . . ." I just lay still and listened to him, wondered what he meant. It was wonderful, but I soon wished he'd stop. I wished I had his feeling for it. It hurts not to be a man sometimes.

"Come on . . ." said the Girl.

"Order him!" snapped the Boy. He was excited about it too. "If we want him to do it, order him to!"

"I did that," said the Girl. "He'll do it."

I heard the Boy stamp away into the darkness. I decided I didn't like him much, all that sudden enthusiasm. I'd have to watch him too, I knew he'd kill me if he could. I didn't hate him or anything, he didn't make me angry. I felt sorry for him really, but I wouldn't let him kill me, not before I did what I was supposed to do.

"All right," I said again. "I'll do it for you. It may not work, but I'll do what you want."

"I'm going down with him," said the Girl.

"You're mad!" said the Boy. "Bitch!" He glared at her. "He's made for it. He'll have resistances, you'll be killed. You can't want it so much!"

"The *stars* . . ." said the Fat Man. "What really are the *stars*? The galaxies, what will they really mean to us? The glory and the reaching out . . ."

"You've got to face it," said the Boy. "You're going to lose him. He's going down where you can't go. Anyway, I'm going to kill him . . ."

"I do what I like! And I won't let you kill him until I've finished my study."

"You still want him! Cow!"

"No . . ." The Girl examined the idea. "No, I don't think so. I've had him . . . But I do want to study him. He's an interesting Android. Perhaps some of his judgement factor could be put into our own machines, the new ships we'll need to build when we get the Engines . . ."

"Just don't stand too near when I come for him!"

"It'll be dangerous for you," I broke in. "I can't take that responsibility . . ."

"I order you to take me," said the Girl, so I couldn't argue any more.

"You'll bring the Toroids?" said the Fat Man. "You'll help us?"

113

"First I must stop the Engines . . ." I liked it. I liked helping people. There was a glow about it, I didn't want to report anyone any more. The Teachers didn't matter now that I knew my Purpose. They'd really be my enemies now, it was their job to see the Machines continued, to see that the world went on and the Matter Engines didn't stop.

The Fat Man nodded. He looked one last time at the consoles then leaned forward and unfastened the things from my head and chest. He swivelled back on his stool, waved with his toothpick and the bands that held me coiled back. I stood up, stretched my legs, felt the silky power of my muscles. It was good to be free, I felt three inches taller.

We walked together from the table across the warm darkness of the metal room. For a few minutes they watched me carefully, kept a few paces away. Fear, I thought. Fear and respect of the Purpose of the Great Robot.

But people had nothing to fear from me. I wouldn't hurt them, I never had, I'd never killed anyone. It was the *systems* I was death to. The failed governments, the powers and principalities. Individual men are all right, it's when there's a group arrogant enough to dare to rule and decide, that's when things go bad. It's the powers that do the mad, bad things, the ones that really *hurt*, they were the things I was against.

Soon K came closer, they all seemed to forget that I was who I was then, they were soon speaking to me as if I was a man. I could forgive anything now I knew what I was for, it was all forgiveness on my side. The Girl took my arm to show me where the door was. When she touched me, that made my brain tingle too. I looked at her and remembered how we'd been before. It was a good memory, and she'd really shown herself while we were explaining things, maybe she'd loved me then. In that Cottage, when we were together there, that hadn't been so bad either.

We went out of the metal room but we didn't go into a Cottage. We stepped on to a circular ramp there that curved around to meet itself coming back. I saw screens that were projecting views of the world from space. When I looked hard there was some small movement in the cloud, I could see the surface down there, the puddle seas all squared off and angular, here and there the original mountains poked through, all rugged and fissured against the relative perfection of the surface.

"Where are they?" I turned and the Fat Man was beside me, trying to see what I was staring at on the screens. "Where are the Matter Machines?"

"In the roots of the World." Down there somewhere. Deep down, I knew but I couldn't describe it. It would have been pointless to try to tell him. Maybe he thought he could get maps and I could show him on them. But that wasn't the way I knew.

They kept on asking me things all the time. I answered as well as I could. We went on down that echoing ramp and at last there was another door. When we went through that we were in a Cottage then.

"See . . ." said the Fat Man. "We can help you too."

"I'll get ready." The Girl went out the way we'd come in and left us waiting there. Time passed, after a while I gave myself a tube.

The Fat Man watched me split my sleeve and roll it up. I didn't care who saw me any more, it didn't matter now that they knew about me. I just put the nozzle into the slot and squeezed. The Fat Man shook his head and laughed.

"I thought the Teachers had you hooked on drugs to use you," he said.

"Food," I said. But he'd guessed that. I didn't eat, obviously, I had to get energy from somewhere. "Disguised," I said. "Camouflage . . ."

"So the Teachers kept you going. Even though you were the Machine that was to destroy their world? Lucky they didn't know."

"Not necessarily, maybe they did know." Who can tell what the Teachers knew or thought they knew? "My tubes were just a part of their ritual, they did it blindly . . ." Maybe they'd known my name, I sure expected to get it from them. They had that code to trigger me all the time, just like these people.

"Perhaps it was the Teachers who failed." The Man

rubbed his chin. "They should have given you your code before."

He was right about that anyway. I'd wanted my name for a long time before I'd got it. I suppose when I realised how bad things were, that was when I started wanting my name.

"But they didn't know you were the Great Robot, they thought that was something else?"

"If they'd thought of it they'd have killed me." It was almost funny. Living under that black shadow all my life, fearing him, setting out to look for him, sending my dog to sniff people in case they weren't human—and all the time it was me!

"They'll think of it now," said the Fat Man. "They're searching for you now, you be careful!" He was right about that too. They had to know by now, that time at the Rites they'd almost guessed. It'd only have taken a little research to find out for sure. They'd certainly want to stop me, they had a place in their world and they'd want it to go on. That's what they were for.

"Thank you," I said. He patted my arm. I saw how his face was grey, how old he looked. I knew I'd do my best for him.

"If you can't get the Toroid—if that's too dangerous, or if it's impossible—still, a record will do. Diagrams . . ."

"When I see it I'll know. I can remember then." I could too. I could record perfectly now, my recall was absolute, the things I forgot were the ones I didn't want to remember.

"Of course. But if you can get one . . ."

"Yes . . ." I'd do that for him. If he ordered me I'd do anything, he knew that. I was made to take orders and to enjoy it. We stood looking at each other, waiting for the Girl to come, waiting for her to get ready. It seemed like a long time.

When she did come she was dressed like me. Her rubbers were made with hemispheres that poked out for her breasts and they were new, but otherwise they were the same. She wore one of those fly-belts in the hooks around her waist, she had a pistol on one side and she had a small pack clipped on the other to balance it. There was a light, transparent helmet hanging under her chin, but I never had one of those.

She didn't sit down. She just asked what we were waiting for.

"You'd better have one of these," said the Fat Man. He went across the Cottage, opened the locker there and gave me a fly-belt out of it. Then he took his own pistol and gave me that too. I mean—his *own* pistol!

"OK?" said the Girl. The Fat Man went to the wall consoles. The Cottage flicked and wavered in the old familiar way, the Man began to check the screens there. The Boy went and opened the curtains a little, he peered out, left and right. When he turned back he nodded to the Man.

"Why don't you go to the stars on the Cottages? What do you need Probes for?" I'd get the Toroids of course— they'd told me to—but I don't like to see people do things the hard way.

"You've got to go there first," said the Girl. "Fool! Android!"

She didn't even look at me. The Boy tittered. I could have bitten my tongue off.

"Good Luck," said the Fat Man. He nodded, the Girl turned to me, it was time to go. I didn't believe in Luck of course, not any more, if I ever did. I told myself there was only calculation and measurement and right and wrong. It was night all the same, a nice thought. I smiled at the Fat Man and he smiled back. The Girl put her hand to the door and we went out.

It was that first Cottage. The original one that had been bombed, all that time ago when I first met the Fat Man and his cat. It was the same place and it was raining and it was dark. I altered my eyes and recognised the churned ashy ground, the twisted, burned aeroplane, the craters and the scattered, washy clay. I fell into one of the craters and the Girl laughed at me.

"They won't expect us here," she said. "They might hear *you*, but they won't expect us." She took the lead and plugged her belt on to her head. "All our entrances are watched, the Teachers know who you are, and probably

117

that you're activated. Her belt started buzzing as she rose. I sorted myself out and followed her up the slope.

We went past that Speaker on its twisted, rusting tripod. There was a new one shining beside it. Someone had slapped mud over the lenses and there was an old helmet perched there like before. When I looked I could see that the helmet was a forgery, something that only looked like rotten steel. I laughed then.

While we were crossing the tumbled bricks from the kiln chimney I looked back to the Cottage and it was in ruins —but that was just another illusion.

"We keep them open," said the Girl. "When they think they're destroyed we can use them."

Later that night we struck some lichen woods and then the moon came out. It was almost good to see those big spiders again and to know I was out of the illusions and lies, back in the real world again.

The further we went on the less Streets there were. It was a deserted sort of place. The farms looked good enough. Maybe the people hadn't even heard of the Rites, perhaps they'd found a way to do without the nutrient, but I didn't really believe that. We were sure out in the wilds, but you could still hear the music.

In one place the landscape had subsided a hundred or hundred and fifty feet—it varied, it wasn't perfect. There didn't seem to be any machines trying to repair it, it was all overgrown down there, it looked as if it had happened a long time ago. The trouble was the world had got too big for the Machines to manage properly. It was all going down, maybe that was why I'd got my name, it was time to make a change.

Dawn came spreading its grey stain across the black sky and the sodden country. The ground where we were was high and you could see Cascades on the square, laid out coastline, to the west.

"Not too far inland," said the Girl. We dropped down to skim the grass and when the sun came up we came to the mountain. I never saw anything like that.

CHAPTER THIRTEEN

IT WAS THE *size* of it—I'd never been close to a mountain before. It was just a big pile of rocks, it went up to the sky, right up to the clouds and into the blue darkness of that morning. North and south you could see other mountains. A chain of them, the Girl said, mostly they were buried in the surfaces. When the sun came up you could see the snow shine pink between the clouds.

When we got near, the world ended. The ground just stopped in a vertical cliff a mile from the tumbled rocks and grass and trees. Right opposite us there was a glacier with water dripping and running off it, there was mist forming where the warmer air hit the ice. That crazy surface of hard rocks, the small pines, it all took on a quality of mystery and recession, a quality of atmosphere. Left and right you could see the structures that supported the surface and the boxy ante-chambers off the Streets. It curved away and back again as it followed around to ring the mountain, from three hundred feet below us it was heavily overhung.

"Beautiful . . ." said the Girl. "*Picturesque*, they'd have called it, like a picture . . ."

First I thought she was talking about the structures, but she meant the mountain. It just looked ugly to me. All that jumble, all that nature. I grunted. An Android isn't expected to make aesthetic decisions, he doesn't have to do things like that. Anyway, I didn't want to argue and make delay.

When she'd looked for a while we hovered out over the edge and moved into the mysteries of the misty trees and rocks. There were jackdaws and ravens, black and tumbling against the sky. They flew up at us, mobbed us. You could hardly hear yourself think, but they left when we landed.

"A waterfall . . ." The Girl consulted her toothpick.

"That's what we've got to find. That'll be where we go down."

We found the place, like a white ribbon falling through spray and rainbows and made it that way. I was happy to let the Girl lead. I had my own way down, but that was ancient, no doubt my landmarks were lost. I certainly wasn't supposed to go near any mountains and I didn't like it between those wet, uncouth boulders, under those dark granite cliffs. It was all *disordered* there and it wasn't right—not natural to me—all that unkempt stone. When we started to get near the Engine, there was to be a particular way I had to go then. I knew I'd be happier when there was only one sure way to go.

Where the water hit the mountain it had cut a deep pool. The water bubbled out and ran away under the City, into the structures and Streets.

While the Girl checked her toothpick I looked back up across the mountain to the surface rim beyond it. There were elegant girders and tracery there, massive pillars evenly spaced beyond the veils of mist. On the close ones, when I turned, there were mosses and cracks, erosion, uneven stresses, a slight bowing of girders and beams. I caught a whiff of rotten nutrient in there somewhere, but I still preferred the structure to the haphazard mountain. I said as much to the Girl but she sneered and said the mountain had logic too, that she could see it and I was only an Android with no soul.

Up on the mountain there were the remains of palaces in the flatter places. Fragments of walls, broken plastic shells, holes maybe, arched caves which had been cellars once. Where the slopes were steeper there were sometimes piles driven in, occasionally they still supported sagging floors. On one place there were stone and mud huts like bee hives and a few people living in them. They had goats about the place, some sheep too, but I didn't see any Dispensers and there were no Speakers either. The only music came faintly from our left.

When K was ready we moved down the slope and into the structures. It was still dusk on the mountain, even though the sun was high it was dark and wet, the tree trunks were black with water. We went weaving through them until we reached the first pillars. The Girl checked her pistol, looked at me, then put on her helmet.

"You ready?" She looked even more beautiful with her gold hair bunched up and flattened behind that clear dome helmet. "We go down here, look out for Teachers!"

We went down quickly. Soon daylight was just a smudge behind us. We kept low on the mountain, the belts guided us through the rocks and dead trees there. There was wreckage once in a while, smashed things, one or two aeroplanes and stuff like that, but the belts just hopped us through. There were more of the palaces too, the same as above, but better preserved because they were protected by the surface.

The Girl would keep stopping in those places and I'd have to wait while she measured and recorded. They seemed to have had rooms or whole buildings for individual people, the Girl hovered through them, comparing walls and dimensions. She said it all meant something to her science.

There were bones sometimes. Shattered ribs . . . bullets, I suppose, or maybe kicking. Once upon a time someone had hung himself in a back porch there. The skull was still suspended on what was left of a wire. The rest of the bones were piled on the stained floor beneath. I don't suppose there'd been any wind there since they roofed it over.

Like before the rooms had screens in them. Mostly they were out, but one or two were still lit and running, all of them were fixed so that you could turn them off if you wanted. We went past the ghostly figures of ancient entertainers, moving in eternal stupid dances as their records ran on, we heard the unending drone of their voices as they flattered each other to the deserted palaces.

Sometimes the Girl got really excited and ran about pointing her toothpick at everything. Once in a while she would stop, pick something up and slip it into her pouch. Souvenirs, I supposed, but in the end I'd had enough. We couldn't waste time like that and I told her we had to move. She scowled at me, but she came. Hell, she knew there were important things I had to do.

Further on there were places where Streets had sagged and the structures had partly fallen on to the mountain.

Sometimes it was so low we had to crouch, twice we had to turn off our belts and crawl through under the breaking concrete.

After a last long scramble we got on to what the Girl called 'the foot hills' and it was a lot easier there. There were lights in the distance and then we hovered up on to what was the roof of the first City and it was practically smooth. The country followed the contours of the original surface so maybe it looked a lot like it did when Earth was Eden, before they built the first city and made it into the second surface.

We hovered through those low, repeating hills, amongst the pillars and Streets where they punched through in their melted holes, the water dark down there. We skirted the occasional light, avoided the few places where the music was loud and the Speakers active. We moved in the shadows, under the radiating beams, flitted like moths in the empty valleys. Sometimes there'd be poor white plants struggling up close to the lights, but they only made the place look worse. It was a good place to think of dying worlds and populations.

The Girl found the stream again and we followed it down between the hills. On the way more water joined it and it cut deeper and deeper into the ground. It was almost a river when it fell off the City edge and into the sea.

"Even concrete wears away," said the Girl.

"It's almost the same as everything else," I said. "Atoms and molecules, it's all the same."

Then we had to wait on the empty shore while the Girl fed herself. There wasn't much to look at, only the sea, disturbed here by the river and the buildings crumbling behind us, rooms laid open like dark trenches. In front there was a bank of pebbles, all different shapes, rounded and mostly white. I'd counted them and started to classify them by shape when the Girl said she was ready and we went on.

She buzzed up on her belt and let out over the ocean and into the darkness. The Streets and pillars reared up out of the water, they were eroded and looked like bottles upside down. When we got out a gentle swell developed, just a slight movement that hardly disturbed the mirror surface of the water. The tide rose as we crossed but it wasn't like the water on the surface near the Cascades, it got rough there when the wind blew.

Then there were many lights ahead and the Streets and pillars got thicker. We threaded into their shadows. I wanted to slow up, but K laughed at me and said it'd be all right. When I thought about it, I could see the lights ahead weren't like the Teachers'. They were brighter, almost like daylight. The Girl seemed to know what was happening so I followed on.

Beyond the pillars there was a raft. A big thing, made of white metal cylinders with flat floors of the same metal fused down on to them. The lights were bright there and the whole thing was heavy loaded, the surface almost awash. I couldn't see any people, but every section was stamped 'Exploration Corps'.

A hundred yards on a pile of something was covered and masked with soft, thick plastic. You could almost see the shapes underneath, but the cover was too thick and not quite transparent. There was row upon row of similar parcels behind the first one, rank on rank of seried packages, some big and some small, mostly they were fifty or a hundred feet tall and just as long.

Closer in I saw the first one had 'TAJ MAHAL Sect IV(a)' stamped on under the Corps marking.

"They're all here," said the Girl. "The Tower of London, the Empire State, the arch from Wells Cathedral . . ."

It was very quiet. There should have been someone about. I put my hand on my pistol, made sure the second one was still under my rubbers. Every time we passed a parcel rank I looked left and right along the aisles. We should have seen Teachers by then.

"Ford," said the Girl. "Most of Detroit, white buildings and fountains . . . collected body styles, the Capitol from Rome . . . the Sphinx . . ."

We went slower and I liked it better. The Girl wanted to look at all the parcels and to touch most of them. Sometimes I thought I saw things move in the light haze amongst the massed packages.

"The Sydney Opera House!" The Girl's voice grew shrill. She flung her arms about in great gestures, she was really excited about those old things. "The Alhambra . . . the Junter Munter . . . the Panama Canal . . . !" I wished she'd stop shouting. "Venice . . . the Eiffel Tower, the Parthenon!" They were all there . . . but hell! They were only stones!

"London Bridge—we've got that! Lascaux . . . a part of a slave by Michelangelo!" Those things moving in the distance, they were *Teachers*! The Girl just went on shouting. "A Cezanne . . . half a Rembrandt!"

They were ahead too. I screwed my eyes and saw them clearly, consulting the arms on their chairs. I got the Girl and spun her to go left. They were there as well.

I got my pistol and dragged the Girl down under a parcel that had 'GREAT BUDDHA, Los Angeles, 2021, buttocks, sect VII(e)' on it.

"The Pentagon," yelled the Girl. "The Kremlin, Edinburgh Castle!" One of the Teachers fired in the air for attention and she giggled.

The Teacher waved his empty hands for me to see and I could hear him telling his friends to keep back. The light was brilliant on his shining lead face. I didn't think I'd have anything to lose talking.

'GREAT ROBOT!' he yelled and came nearer. "We know who you are and what you're supposed to do. We . . . we will *help* you . . ." The Girl giggled again and I knew he was lying too.

"How did you find us?" If I could keep him talking there'd be a chance to get through. There were more Teachers coming all the time.

"You're part of the Deep Machine, you're the Great Robot, the Machine knows now . . ."

"Whitehall," said the Girl. "Canberra . . ."

"So it follows the Machine can trace you. It knows its own, it knows your thoughts and where you are. You're a part of it, Candy Man!"

"I've got to turn it off. That's my *Purpose*!"

"The Machine's function is to continue . . ."

The Girl giggled again. I kept a tight hold on her. I could feel her shaking as she laughed. Hysteria, I thought. I couldn't understand her.

"The Machine must finish."

"That's what *you* want. You're only a part of it, the ceasing mechanism. The *whole* Machine is made to continue . . ."

I thought I could perhaps blow a hole in the raft, dive down and escape that way. I could shoot lights out first, I might get away with it. The Girl got a hand free, tightened the neck seal of her helmet.

"Stalingrad . . ." she said. "Vimy Ridge . . . Passchendaele, Bataan, Chicago . . ."

One of the Teachers fired. Nerves, I suppose, they're only human. A yard of plastic splashed off the stone behind me. The great parcel rocked and Buddha dust sprayed down on to my neck. The Girl wriggled free and disappeared.

"Sedgemoor, Glencoe . . . Tel El Kebir . . ." Her voice was somewhere near, but I didn't dare look.

The nearest Teacher wheeled desperately back, firing as he went. The floor ripped open in front of me. Hot water splashed up, I fired near that Teacher and then I frightened another. I hated to do it, but I couldn't let them stop me, I'd gone too far by then. I had to take chances like that, I believe I'd have killed to get through.

I crouched up under the overhang of the Buddha's belly firing when the Teachers came too near. Up above the Girl was still shouting names and laughing. She was far away, sitting up there on the flat top of the Buddha's hips —where they'd cut the sculpture off to move it easier. She didn't flinch or move when the charges cracked past. I suppose the Teachers were shooting at me, not her. Maybe that's why she thought it was so funny.

The smoke got thicker all the time. Soon I couldn't see the Teachers at all and from where they were shooting they couldn't see me either.

"Polaris," said the Girl. "Short magazine Lee Enfield, Me 163 , , , mace . . ."

The Teachers got a hold on themselves. There were some shouted orders and they started shooting at the Buddha. Maybe they could see the top over the smoke. They blasted stone out all around my ears and it was time to go.

I ignored the flames and crawled through the plastic

125

until I was against the stone. It was easy. There was a trench torn through the Buddha's thigh. It was hot in there, but it was cooler when I got round to the back.

I forced on underneath the plastic into a deep, rounded crevice. The sides were polished smooth and it was hard to get a grip but I managed to worm up to where K was. I got my knife and made a cut so that I could tear the plastic open.

The Girl was peering down into the smoke over the swelling plastic covered belly. Looking for me, I suppose. When I struggled out she turned and then fell over laughing. Smoke got down her throat and she almost choked coughing.

I put my knife away, reached down and took her round the waist. She didn't do anything, she didn't even try to get up. My belt carried us both up out of the smoke and gunfire.

After a minute she put her arms up and hung on my neck. Her face pressed up to mine behind her helmet. Even through our rubbers I could feel her body, or maybe I imagined it.

She didn't make a movement to use her own fly-belt. Then she stopped smiling and just looked at me; I thought she was going to kiss me until I remembered that helmet. Right then I wished I was a man again and we were back in the Cottage, but that thought soon went.

"Hiroshima . . ." She said that like it ought to mean something. "If you turn off the Machine the race will be free again. Have you thought of that? Of what it'll mean . . . of what it might mean?" Right then I could hardly think of anything. I kept saying in my head that I was an Android, they did say I was made like a man and I certainly felt like it.

"No . . ." I hadn't considered what might happen. She wrapped her legs around my right thigh.

"Free to do what they like to themselves, free to do it all again . . ." I hadn't seen her like that before. Concern was strange from her, she seemed to see what I was thinking. "Oh yes, sex is my pleasure—any sex—but you can't have even that if everybody's dead. The suffering too, I don't like to think of the race's history, them all

126

going through that again. My Brother . . . he's the one that needs violence . . ."

"I must stop the Machines." That was the thing, the *one* thing. The great point of it all—you've got to fulfil your Purpose. What men made of things after was their business.

She moved herself closer, laughed again. She put out her tongue at me, moved her body against my chest. She was playing like she always was, I never saw her serious again, not after that.

CHAPTER FOURTEEN

I MOVED THROUGH the lower beams with the Girl under my arm and wondered why the Teachers had let me get away with it. It seemed strange to hunt me down like that and then let me slip through, but then, you never had much real trouble getting away from Teachers, sometimes they just seemed to forget.

"They never look up," said the Girl. "Teachers never look up, do they?" I said I'd noticed that before.

I could see them down there in the smoke, converging between the parcel ranks, shooting at the Buddha. There was heavy smoke down there, moving like a slow river in the still air; the confusion grew with the shooting.

"They'll ruin that statue," said the Girl. "Just think of the damage they're doing! All the priceless things!" She got angry, I thought she was going to ask me to go down and stop it. When she opened her mouth to speak again I scowled, so she said nothing. We moved on then, before the Teachers had time to think.

It was twenty miles before we came to the end of the parcel raft. It was low in the water, almost awash with treasures. Sometimes there were shallow pools with dark seaweed in them. There was life in the Old Seas, all they needed was a little light. As we went on there were still more pillars, all set in round holes, so the raft could rise and fall with the tide. The World was becoming denser, like it was around the Rites, you could tell there was something important ahead.

Then we hit land. Saw it in the distance. When I looked first I thought it was another mountain. I searched my memory but I couldn't place anything like that near the Machines. I began to wonder if the Girl had led me wrong.

Closer it didn't look so big. It was just a ridge really, two hundred feet high in places, masked and partly hidden by the pillars. The parcels stretched away beneath us, object after object, all neatly arranged for storage. I watched the ridge come up—and then light shone yellow through it, dark shadows moved inside as our position changed. It was parcels. A great wall of plastic packages.

"The West coast of the Old Atlantic," said the Girl. "They probably had a name for it. The Streets are thickest from here on. We have to cut down the Artifacts to get them to where we can lift them. Anastylosis, that's called. You can't mess about too much with the Streets, disturb the Anti-Gravity—the World might fall down."

The shadowed cliffs and waxy transparencies of the parcel wall spun beneath us as we crossed over. There was another ten miles before we got clear of that and all the way the Girl recited long lists of names. It didn't have the magic it had before. She wasn't so excited the second time and she didn't move me as she had.

Beyond the parcels the land started. There wasn't much difference. It was as flat as the raft and it was divided up in the same way, except the slabs weren't metal floats, but great flags of concrete. Here and there were rounded heaps of grassy earth, as if someone had been clearing it and never finished. The Streets ended too, it was just a vast open space. There were sun lights all over the sky. The Girl told me we'd left the Sea but I knew that anyway, I'd started to remember again.

"It took centuries to get our Artifacts—I still can't believe we've got them all." She waved an arm back across the plastic. "Everything worth having—we *ought* to have everything."

There were Rockets ahead. Big ones. Some sitting on their bellies, the great dumb-bell nuclear ships, older ones standing up on their tails to beg. A city of them, as thick as the pillars ever were, all the varied shapes, the vast sizes, all wrapped in their layered plastic.

Steam or white smoke plumed up amongst them. It all looked like some spired, medieval city in the misty valley of its morning. Test wires and feeds snaked bright coloured all across the ground. On the horizon you could see bright red fire and towering smoke from a test run, later the thunder reached us too. I wondered what 'medieval city' was, what exactly spires were for.

"Why not use the Cottages? Why bother with planetary Rockets when you can transmit matter?" Sometimes I thought I'd never understand what the Corps did.

"We do. It's the *power* it takes, the range is limited. A slow job with just the Cottages anyway. The Rockets themselves are Artifacts—very worthy ones. We use them to transport themselves, or we will. It means we can use the Anti-Gravity too, send them up the Streets. Some things we don't like to cut up to put in the Cottages."

"Where are you taking all this stuff?"

"Now, when we have the *Toroid*, all the power that means, then we can make bigger Cottage mechanisms. Then we'll do *everything*—anything at all then!"

"But where do you take the Artifacts?" She flashed a look at me, then turned her head away. She hesitated. "Is it a secret?" I could always threaten to leave the Toroid if she wouldn't tell.

"To our . . . our *Fleet*. Our satellite stations . . . station. The Ship we came home in. Where we came from. No harm in telling you. When we get the Toroid it'll solve everything, it'll all be different then."

In one place some men were clearing the covering off an upright Rocket. Great sheets of it were peeled away, left lying on the paving like old, giant snake skins. The revealed metal shone like silver, but you could see places where it had turned grey.

"Checking them out," said the Girl. "Of course, we haven't actually tried to use one yet, just the test runs—they're in a bad condition. They're from the very first days in space, all of them. Not even made of concrete, most of them."

She had me land then and we separated. We went on foot then, walked quickly across the paving. The Girl was a lot more cautious. All the time she was switching her head about, but I couldn't see any sign of Teachers. She walked a yard to my right and I let her lead. She wasn't relaxed, she didn't smile any more. Her lips were compressed, she had a sort of pride, a quality of determination and authority.

The work people were women as well as men and they were all in Corps uniform, except one or two who were working on fuel systems and had rubbers like ours. They looked pretty small up on the gantrys and ladders, the small power tools flashed in their hands.

A gang rolling up striped plastic stopped talking as we passed and they all turned to watch us go. Nobody said anything, the Girl didn't even look at them. Some of the men took off their caps and they all seemed to be wiping their hands on dirty rags.

"Why not put Machines to it? Why put men to do things machines could do as well?"

"Cheaper to make. They don't cost the Crops anything, in a way you're worth a thousand men, Candy . . ."

"Training . . . that must cost . . ."

"We don't train them." Teachers maybe, I thought.

"What about this place? Did the Corps make it?"

"Yes." The Girl turned to me. "Why do you ask?"

"I've got to find out where to look for the Machines, the Engine." That wasn't exactly true, I knew where to go. Why should I tell *her* everything? After what she'd done to me? I knew I could always find the Engines.

"Yes, yes. The Corps made this place. But long before it was called the Corps. Right back when there were 'nations', right back before they thought of the World City —of if they thought of it they didn't believe it!" She smiled to herself, looked around. "Long before your time, Candy Man!"

"They left it here when they made the first Surface?"

"Yes. It was cheaper. When the Machines kept on building they just roofed it over. They launched Rockets up the Streets, assembled the big Ships in space. When we came it was like it is now.'

"The men?"

"The men too. They haven't launched a Rocket for a thousand years, but they ran the place, kept it up. The Machines train the men, the people the Teachers pass into the Corps. A self sufficient thing. A law to itself, they got all the good blood that came along in the Rites. It's the main thing, the Pads, the Rocket Plain, the Corps base on Earth, everything else is a concealment, what you'd call camouflage. Everything is for *us*, what it's really about was keeping a place fit for us, keeping everything for when *we* came home . . ."

"The Saver . . ."

"Ah . . ." She brightened. Her scientist face came on again. She began to take notes on her toothpick. "You know that myth? Still surviving, but now mixed with the memory of the Corps? Do you think the people think of us as the Saver?"

"The Saver wasn't going to be like you!" He sure wasn't, that prophecy was nothing to do with our business! I wondered how, even when I was a man, how I could ever have thought it might have been him that I was dealing with. "Nothing to do with us," I said, more quietly. "That's something else."

"All right . . ." The Girl looked down. "Maybe I'll ask someone else . . ."

"Especially it's nothing to do with you!"

"No, I didn't mean that . . ." She changed the subject. "You know that this is the actual, the *real* surface?"

"*What?*"

"Yes." she couldn't have known, of course, but there was only one place like that—and that was where the Matter Engine was. The place of the Deep Machines! I'd thought it was still a long way away. That Rocket testing started again. K's helmet glinted with the red fire from it, we shouted above the thunder.

"Are you sure?"

"Yes." She looked at me curiously. "Yes, only think, six feet under here, beneath the concrete, there's the original paving! And under that there's real filling, and then *soil*! It goes on to *bedrock*! Over there—under the parcels—that's where they filled the ocean shallows. Think of *that*!"

I screwed my eyes, began to scan the paving slabs. The Girl kept on talking.

"So close to nature. Think of the days when they grew things, mated cattle for food!" I grunted and kept on looking at the slabs.

To the west, between white plumed Rockets, there was a low hill. I recognised its shape, saw the writing on it, those symbols—the mottoes they used to send me wrapped around my tubes. I should have known that hill before, should have recognised the compound curve of its slope long before. Too long a man, I supposed. I hoped the machines would know me still.

I found where the pattern started in the paving, put my feet in the first position. I stood there a long time, looking at the hill, rocking the right amount and studying the pattern, remembering what I must do. The Girl was standing right behind me.

"I must go this particular way," I said without turning.

"This is *it*? Are we near the Engines?"

"You follow me exactly." As I spoke that prick came in my brain. It was like before, like with the Teachers and with the Fat Man.

"I'm not doing anything for an Android!" She got angry again. "I'm not doing what you tell me. You say where the Engines are!"

"Do as you're told! Do as I do!" I started walking. She couldn't see the things that I could and she didn't like it. She didn't understatnd the importance of doing every small thing just right. I was proud of my Purpose, it was the most important thing of all and now the Corps depended on me.

I found the next of the sixty-four positions. I moved on carefully through the complicated patterns that no one else in the world could see. The concrete was brilliant and hot in the sun lights, the lines between the slabs led over the hill, perfect in their perspective. I went quickly through the acts, the Girl had to struggle to keep up and that was her hard Luck because she was only human. Then she got in front and turned to look up into my face.

132

"Don't tread on the lines!"

'What? Afraid the bears'll get you?" Her lip curled. "Is it *here*? Tell me!"

"Worse than bears. Where else would it be?"

"The Rocket Plain! We found nothing!"

"Under it. Tunnelled under and nobody told." We Machines could keep our secrets. "Get back in line, follow *me*. Don't spoil the code!" She was quiet then, she'd seen the expression on my face. She followed at a distance, determined to miss nothing, trying to learn it all.

"You can't come in. You can't approach the Machine, let alone the Engine. You must wait outside, I'll bring you the Toroid."

"I *can*! I can go everywhere!" I didn't argue. There was no time for distractions. She could go on for a while, but in the end she'd have to stop.

At the foot of the hill the doors opened when they saw me coming. The Girl gasped, they'd been invisible before, except to me. I told her how nothing was simple, how everything was either disguised or an illusion. I went to the last place and did the last things.

I entered. The Girl followed. It didn't really matter yet, so I let her come. The walls were twenty feet apart and you could see the marks where the green concrete had been cast against a heavy grained wood.

Thirty paces on more doors opened. Two sentries in chromium helmets brought up small rifles and saluted. There was fine white dust on their shoulders and cheekbones, they hadn't moved for years. I suppose they were Androids—you'd have to call them that—but they were inferior, hardly more than robots. They were identical for one thing, made from moulds, not grown like me. They fell in behind and we went through the doors.

It was all activity in there. We were on a balcony that ran around the place so we could see everything. Girls in short grey skirts, and big, pointed breasts ran about with handfuls of paper and tapes. Speakers buzzed, men sweated while they answered. Diminishing numbers flashed between tall screens, lights and codes twinkled. The men were all absorbed, working hard behind their ranked consoles. They didn't give us a glance, they had hardly

133

seen us come in. The Girl arrived beside me and I heard her gasp.

"Control Room!" she said. "They should have told us! You can't trust them!"

The dwindling numbers reached zero. There was a thunder like the crack of doom behind us. I looked up and all the screens were filled with a big Rocket firing.

It was on the Plain out there. The same place, I saw the slabs and the perspective of the lines. The Girl's mouth sagged open; we watched the Rocket go up on the thunder glory of its engines.

"*God!*" whispered the Girl. "After all this time . . ." The Rocket climbed like a pointing finger, penetrated the smoke, rose steady through it. It was a fine mechanism, it was ancient but it was also an ultimate work of the race's art. An expression of their vitality, that they had *lived* . . . of the strength of their Purpose when they were young, before we Machines arrived. The Girl was more angry than ever.

"They should have told us! Oh! That *Rocket!*" We watched the splendid thing go, saw the white fumes streaming from its vents. Slowly, it gained speed so *slowly*. In the Control Room the noise was unbelievable. The Girl had her hands over her ears, she was screaming, tears were running down her face. On the Control Room floor they were screaming too.

The noise slackened. The Rocket was a point of fire through the clouds. The Girl stood with clenched fists, she writhed with anger and excitement.

"Oh . . . the Rocket . . . perfect! They should have told us they had one ready. If they've damaged it . . . !"

There was something wrong. Something different about those big screens. I stepped back three paces and looked through the doors to the light outside. I laughed then.

Nothing moved on the Rocket Plain. There was no mighty smoke cloud, nothing stirring. The Rocket in the screens moved out against the perfect blue sky; it gleamed and vanished into a sunburst in the lenses. There was no sun like that on the Plain, the colour was different and the light was duller. It lacked the reds of the real thing—the parcels weren't there either. I turned and grinned at K.

134

"Don't laugh at me—you dirty Android!"

"GO! GO BABY!" The Corps men on the floor were still shouting their magic words.

"Illusions," I said. "To fool themselves and to fool you and fool you again!" You couldn't believe anything in the world, *anything*. She should have known that. Antithesis was as good as thesis, what difference when everyone was fooled? I didn't mind, I'd thought I was a man and I wasn't. I didn't care what she called me, I didn't mind not being a man. I didn't mind being an Android.

"Like *you*! You half-man!" I made myself keep on smiling. The Girl stopped mouthing and just frowned at me.

"Camouflage," I said. "What isn't an illusion is camouflage. That Rocket, just some old record."

"You know everything! Damned Android!"

"You sure you've really got the Taj Mahal? Sure it's really Porton Down and not just plastic? Sure that bull cave you've got from Lascaux isn't a lithograph?" I fought my anger, looked away from her down the Control Room. "If you don't know what you're doing, you should ask someone."

The Rocket was gone now. The men turned to shout congratulations at each other. Arms waved and they hugged each other, laughing all the time.

"Boy . . . real *bird*!"

"Perfect! Like last time!"

"God!" said the Girl. "Probably the same record! The same for a thousand years!" Nobody heard her. We grinned at each other, the anger forgotten.

As I got nearer the Machines I felt better, more confident. The Girl was right. I remembered everything and I knew everything—or anyway, all I needed to know.

We went round the balcony above the gesturing people. They ignored us, maybe they didn't see us because they didn't expect to. The papers were dancing down there and the champagne bottles were popping. We came to steps and went down there. Even when we were amongst them the people didn't see us.

Wine foam splashed into my face. It was cold and that

135

was nice, I laughed to be like the rest of them. It was good to be near the Engine.

"You Androids all together!" The Girl dashed away the glass someone offered her. "You can laugh! You're not real either!"

"They're not Androids!" How could she have thought they were? We don't drink wine, not for pleasure anyway. "They're your people. Corps Men!"

"They should have told us! We discovered them polishing that Plain! They ought to have told us! The Control Room—the Engine down here!"

"You tell them everything? They're smart in their way —they're Corps too!" I ran my tongue round my lips. That wine, it wasn't a bad sensation. I liked it.

"Why should we? All they had to do was collect souvenirs—get the Artifacts."

"Anyway, they don't know about the Engine." That *champagne* . . . that was good . . . "They don't know what's happening, they're just playing out their dreams of Rockets. They're camouflage and they don't know it." Hell, what did it matter as long as I had my Purpose? Who cared who fooled who? Certainly not the people fooled, so long as they were happy.

We were at the back of the room. I felt really Lucky. The party was building up behind us. One of the scientists had taken off her glasses and was dancing on the consoles. There were men falling about and clapping her. I saw wine spray across the master screens.

The roof swooped down to meet the floor. I doubled up and groped under to get my feet in the right place.

Explosive ribbon cracked the entrance out across my shoulders. The noise was lost in the singing from the consoles. The slab across my back weighed nine hundred pounds. I lowered it to exactly the right place on the floor. I did it right and the Machines knew me. I turned to the Girl.

"You . . . you're growing!"

"No—it just looks like that." I got a foot into the entrance. "You must stay here."

"No! This radiation suit . . . my helmet . . ."

"Hold her!" The soldiers slung their rifles and grabbed

136

her. One pinioned her arms and the other got her legs. After a second she stopped struggling and just swore at me.

I put up my left arm, found the hold and swung up into the hole. Only I could go where I was going.

"Please . . ." said the Girl. *"Please,* Candy!"

"You wait." I wondered what it was about the Machines she wanted so; I'd said I'd get them the Toroid. Maybe it was the thought of all that power, all in that dangerous place, those deadly radiations, maybe it excited her.

"You wait," I told K again. I got my head further up into the tunnel. The sound and light cut off and I was alone in the dark.

There was a hesitation as the Machine tested me and then the tunnel sucked me up. It pressed in on me, tried its soft pressure on the contours of my body. It was all right, I enjoyed it, a perfect fit, it was good to be right. I wondered what it'd have made of the Girl.

The Machine moved me upwards. It was tremendous. It was coming home and I was at my Purpose. I knew where I was going and what it would be like when I got there.

CHAPTER FIFTEEN

THE TUNNEL DROPPED me neatly out on to the polished corrugated floor. Before I had time to look around massed jets shot nerve gas all over me. It didn't hurt exactly, but it sure stung my face, and I fell over. That floor wasn't meant for walking on, or not much anyway.

When I'd wiped the stuff from my eyes the first thing I saw was my dog.

Good old Wolf! He knew me without smarting my skin with gas or squeezing me in a tunnel. He knew where to go when he'd lost me, he knew I'd be coming there. His tail waved great friendly arcs and he welcomed me the way dogs do even when they're robots. I grabbed his ears and we laughed at each other.

137

The buzzing in my head rose. It got almost unbearable and then there were patterns in it that I could understand.

"Yes. It is us," said the Deep Machines. Lenses came questing out over and around me. After a while they went away a bit and I could stand up. *"It is satisfactory."* The Machine told me.

"Sit!" Wolf stopped growling at the lens arms and sat beside me. I looked up and down the ranks of squat grey calculator boxes in the pulsing violet light. They weren't as big as I'd expected, they weren't anything like as impressive as I'd remembered.

"Externals. What happens inside is what matters. You are tainted with humanity . . ." I understood all the buzzing now, I was a part of it. I studied the banked flicker of the tiny lights, the pulsed waver of their patterns, the pure white pencil murmur of laser commands across the dark empty receptors. I saw the seats where men had built and tested before humans were no longer necessary.

"Part," said the Machine. *"Your circuit has its function. Go to the master place. Do it quickly."* It was an order.

I suppose, if I'd never been a man, I'd have just gone and done that like I should have. But I was more than a machine, more than a designed number of functions, all dependent on stimulations. Maybe that was why I got words from the Deep Machine, rather than the simple codes it had really sent me. Anyway, I said nothing and kept on going up that dim, brilliant aisle, up that corrugated floor between the massed power of Machines. The Matter Engine was that way and I was going to it. Function or no function, I was going beyond my Purpose and I liked it.

Everywhere lights and lasers flicked at me, played across my cheeks, searching for my eyes. I felt messages brush and vibrate across my hands. Always there was my other voice in my head, always my Machine part ordered me only to the master place.

"DO IT!" It was shouting now, the voice had something that began to sound like anger.

"I want a Toroid. I want the secret of the Matter Engine. That is part of my Purpose now, it has been added."

138

"Not so! Not written in your function! Not on your own program!"

"I have that right of discretion. I can speak of right and wrong, I was made like a man."

The Machine thought about that. I heard it. It thought about it in my head and all around me. The radio, the radiations and lasers spoke a thousand persuasions, a thousand arguments and counter theories. Down there, in that net of our conscious, I was even more a part of the Deep Machine.

"Only the program. There is only the program."

"I will give a Toroid to the Corps. To humanity." I said that. The human part of my brain, that overlay there. "For the race to survive it must grow, it must pioneer. It must go to the galaxies! For that the Corps must have the power of the Matter Engines, we must give them the Matter Engines."

"We. You/us . . . we are the total Machine, a part must not be against the whole!" It was like talking to myself. *"Our decision is total. All there is. The decision. So far as you exist you are only a part, a faulty part."* It was terrible. A half of me said that, but my half knew what it must do for the people it served.

"I am the ender." Ego . . . my human parts . . . the man structure fought back. It was my decision. Mine! "The ender is the stronger. You . . . we . . . *you* must allow me!"

"Total decision!" The arguments came again but I ignored them. I held that Matter Engine in my mind. I forced my way through the commands and arguments down the buzzing click of flickering Machines.

"TOTAL TERMINATION! The program is total termination. Your Purpose! You cannot judge and choose!"

It got harder. I drove my legs, drove my conscious before like a herd of wayward sheep. It was hell. All the time the Machine was shouting in our head.

"All must end or nothing. You wish to change your/our program?" The Machine sounded incredulous. It was incredible, it was ridiculous . . . I knew how it thought . . . who ever heard of a Machine changing its Purpose!

"Yes!" I said, but I could feel myself weakening.

139

"*No . . .*" the voice in my head persuaded. It was *illegal*. I saw that now. I saw the logic. How much simpler it was to stick to Program, to my Purpose! I halted. Maybe the Machine part had won then. Our unity, our program, that was all there was to do.

Wolf ambled past. His paws clicked and slipped on that hard floor. I heard them with my ears. He stopped. Looked back, enquired with his eyes and ears whether we were going on, when we were going on. I woke up then, I knew. I was the master, I had the functions of a man, I was master of the Machine. I had the decision. I was *separate*. Wolf told me. Wolf knew I was separate.

The Machine saw what happened. Even as I stepped forward it tried to kill us. More nerve gas first, the great fool should have known better! Then it arced lightning at me from the screens and tried to cut us up with lasers. It was pretty hot for five minutes but my rubbers took the worst of it. Wolf got his hair singed and he started barking, but he was all right too. You can't kill a robot dog just like that. The Machines didn't have the capacity to hurt us much, they were designed that way I guess.

Then the Machine gave up the physical stuff and got cunning. It still had contact with my mind, it started a bombardment of illusions. The aisle turned into a catwalk. Narrow, with no handrail, that burning lightning playing up and down its length. Rain or nerve gas or something drove stinging into my face. There was gunfire and flame throwers like when the Boy had tortured me. Monsters or things like them leapt up and disappeared before I could strike at them. The Deep Machine was working on my human side now, hitting where it knew I would be weakest.

I suppose I knew it was all illusions, like everything else. But the Machine had more than half my mind and I couldn't stop believing. It's a big trouble when you can't stop believing. Then the catwalk ended in raging ocean and seaweed creamed out of it at my feet, the white belly flash of sharks a little further out. I wanted to stop, so I did.

Wolf walked right out across the water barking all the way against the noise. I knew it'd be OK to follow him. I knew he'd be seeing things clearer than me, but I still couldn't believe it. He turned and pricked his ears at me

140

again. I remembered I couldn't drown anyway and went on after him. When I got his handle I felt through it how he was wondering what was holding me. I guess his mind was too simple to be fooled the way mine was.

I was part of the Deep Machine and Wolf was a part of me. Wolf was my dog, combined through his handle we added up to something else and that was enough to survive the Machine. We went on together and the sea faded back to being catwalk and then to the real corrugated floor.

There was a grey door next. Wood it looked like. A sort of hard, grey wood, pretty near in colour to the concrete it probably was really. The illusions seemed to have cleared, I looked back down the aisle through the quiet ticking of the Machine.

I let Wolf go and he pattered to the door, sniffed there and turned waving his great tail. I came up to the door crushing fat black and pink snakes like up in the woods. I hated them from when I was a man. I don't know why that stupid Machine should think they'd worry an Android. Even though they weren't real I hated them, wriggling fat things, some dirty thing about them, some ancient dirty thing. It was very quiet, even the voice in my head had stopped. I brushed the snakes away and reached for the brass door handle.

The door went up like a shutter and left me reaching for nothing and facing myself.

It looked me right in the eyes. It wasn't a reflection but it took me right back to the mirrors when I'd been so worried. I knew it wasn't a mirror because our hands brushed when we reached for the knob.

He looked almost as surprised as I was but he recovered quicker. He snarled at me. The Machines had made me symmetrical, maybe they did everything like that. Maybe it was a universal law, maybe they had to. If I was made to stop the Machines he was made to keep them going. Go-stop . . . dark-light . . . positive-negative . . . a balance that was necessary, or maybe the Machine knew the horror I had at the thought of there being two of me, or even a reflection. The deep down shock that I was not unique. Wolf barked and hung out his tongue, tried to take us both in.

He smashed at my throat with the side of his hand. His rubbers were better than mine, he had all the gear clipped to him that I must have started with. When he had me on my back and was trying to tear my throat out his face came close and I saw how he was cleaner, how he looked younger, he was fresh from being made, he'd never been a man, he still believed in the Machines.

His fingers left my throat and he tried to put his thumb nails in my eyes. I chopped his waist left and right with both hands. On the third stroke he whined out of his nose and let go.

We rolled apart, whirled and got up. He came for me again. We gave each other blows that'd have killed elephants. He kicked hard at my shin but I bent my knee and stopped his kick in the soft part of his thigh. As I got my foot down he stamped on my instep but I still managed to punch him hard on the forehead. He staggered back a few paces and we began to circle each other.

We both knew what the other could do and that was the trouble. The fight went on and there was never any advantage except his nose was knocked sideways and he'd smashed one of my ears. Wolf was barking and dancing round us all the time and the Machines started playing thunderstorms again and cheering him on.

I made a quick movement and got my pistol but he chopped it right out of my hand. He left himself open doing it so I kicked his legs from under him and dived on him to finish it. He got a foot under my stomach and the next thing I knew I'd crashed through the door and fetched up against the wall in a corner. I lay dazed and thinking I'd have to get up or he'd kill me.

"Turn off the Machines," he said. "You us? There'll be only me now." It was horrible how he looked like me. "I'm going to finish with you. That's my Purpose, to kill the Great Robot and be the Saver. I'll save the Machines . . ." He hesitated. "Maybe I ought to just break your legs and send for the Teachers . . ."

Wolf stopped barking. I saw him cock his head and look back through the doorway. The other me turned too. He had time to open his mouth and in that instant light and fire came through the door and a full charge took him in the chest.

He sprawled backwards, lay there, heavy brown smoke coiled up from him. The Girl came through the door, the pistol still glowing in her hand.

She went to the dead me and knelt down. She took his pack and emptied it, scattered the contents as she searched, her blacked out helmet quested about the floor. She was in a hurry, she talked as she searched.

"Got to get it . . ." She was panting, her voice was muffled inside the helmet, she must have run all the way from the tunnel. "Those radiations." She wasn't talking to anybody, just to herself. I tried to get up and found I couldn't, not then, not yet.

"Not here," said the Girl. "Not here . . . he couldn't have got it . . ." She stood up, looked quickly around, made little jerking motions with her hands. "What to *do* . . . what'll he *say* . . ." For all she knew she'd just wiped out the race's whole hope for the future. "He'll be so *angry*!" I guessed she meant the Fat Man. I pushed myself off the floor and stood up. My pistol was near my feet so I picked it up. The Girl turned, her weapon came up, then she lowered it.

"How . . . ?"

"There were two of us. Why did you come? How did you make it?"

"It's open now. When one's done it anybody can. There are only the radiations, this suit can't protect me for ever. I can't stand here long."

"Come on then!" Hell, I'd done my best for her. She'd got a dose already, having a bit more wouldn't hurt her.

We stepped over the mashed jelly of electronics that had been me and went up the corridor. Wolf sniffed at it, but he came when I called. It's a hell of a thing to see yourself shot down. The corridor was a long one and every ten paces there was a lead wall you had to go round, to protect the Deep Machines from the Matter Engine, I supposed. I knew it got pretty hot where I was going. At last there was a door made of lead slabs and bound with rusty steel. The Girl kept checking readings on her toothpick.

"It's all right," she said. "Not bad at all."

"Maybe the Engines are shut down."

"I stay here, you go on."

I pushed and the door opened for me. The radiations lapped on my face. I heard them with my skin, felt them lance through me. The dog whimpered but we went on. He'd be hurt even less than me, all that hair, it was good protection, I knew he'd be OK unless his piles got magnetised. Anyway, as long as I lasted to get the Toroid it didn't matter.

The room was vast. It'd been lined with the same steel-bound lead—the real stuff, they hadn't had concrete when they'd built this place. Rust ran on the walls, complicated red rusty steel lace that had been four inch armour plate sagged from the ceiling above the consoles. The floor was rusty too, crusty above the lead, our feet crunched as we walked across it. The air was steamy and warm, the concentric rings of light were so many misty halos all amongst the sagging lead ceiling blocks. Somewhere, in all the ultra-sonics from the Matter Engine you could hear water running.

I walked to the dark-light radiating mass that filled the centre of the room. It was the top of the Matter Engine, the rest of it, most of it, reached three hundred feet down. Dead vertical, perpendicular, dead on a line to the earth's centre. The Toroid formed the upper ring of the Engine. It was a hundred yards across. I'd never shift it, the case was rusted solid, anyway it was too big to move through the corridor.

I trained my eyes and started recording. I knew it anyway. Now that I'd been to the Matter Engine I knew its functioning like I understood the Deep Machine. I had it all in my head.

I went and broke away more of the Toroid case. The rings were quite clear. Each a yard across, made up of smaller rings, and each of the smaller made of rings again. Tiny things, right down to a sub-microscopic crystal structure. They were pretty, all winking with light and life. I got my knife and tried to winkle one out, but it was too tough and the blade broke.

Anyway, I told myself, I understood its functioning, the

144

mechanics of it, the patterns that should be on its screens. I went to the consoles, brushed away the fallen rust. Everything was aged and blackened, I could hardly see the figures and readings. It didn't matter, I knew all that, I could hold it in my head.

I found the transfers that plugged the consoles to the Deep Machine. It was all corroded there, but the sensations still flowed. I yanked them out and the Machine yelped. From far away I thought I heard the Girl laugh.

I took the main control to myself, turned and walked back to the crusted rim of the Toroid. I looked over there into the matrix of the Matter Engine.

Space was strange down there. The volume had a denser look towards the centre. The steam droplets looked as big as melons, further down I saw what were molecules of water. It varied too. I saw stars, the black velvet of deep space, oceans and faces from the past and what might have been the future once. Across the Toroid nebulae twisted, a galaxy grew there. I thought I saw time move, and there was some superb thing looking at me, maybe from a similar Engine from some far galaxy, no doubt wondering who I was. I saw the Girl naked in the Cottage, I saw the Potter breaking pots, infinity away I saw a severed Teacher go spinning up a Street.

There was sound too, a sound of music. The colours were beautiful and Wolf's howling became a song of beauty. Columns of ionised gas danced on the edge of the void core of the terrible thing, all the time the power crackled, the radiations beat on my face.

I opened the control with my mind. Matter grew from down there. Thin spider webs of concrete came spinning up from nothing. Space condensed and somehow the centre void was filled. Rainbows danced, stress lines formed zebra patterns black and white on nothing. The thin cobwebs of concrete became thicker, the nothing core grew, matter spun out in pencil thickness, became tree trunks and rivers, spun from grey to pink. I was fascinated, hypnotised. I studied it all, took it into my head.

Wolf was barking, tearing at my heels. From somewhere I heard the Girl yelling for me to cut the radiations. I woke up with a jerk. I'd looked down there too long! A man would have been dead a thousand times within a mile of the thing. I had looked into its heart as if it was my candy machine, already my face was blackened and my eyes were pressing out. I've have to hurry, I was a dying Android.

I closed the Engine. Shut it down to zero, reversed the polarities. I heard the Machine scream like when I'd pulled out its transfers. The lower Toroids came crashing back out of super-light. The steel case burst, sprayed the place with rusty chips of metal. Something ripped like a bullet through my upper arm, but it didn't matter. All the colours flashed and the vacuum of the nothing core sealed with a clap of thunder. The matter skeins waved for a moment and turned from pink to lead grey to fall back down there. As they hit the lower part there was a flash and a crump and a fire ball as they exploded.

Energy briefly torched out of the shaft. The lead roof above melted then vapourised. The floor warped up and thumped back again. I lay still, expecting to be vapourised too but nothing more happened. Most of the energy went back to where the matter had been coming from. I remember hoping that the superb thing that had watched me hadn't got all that explosion suddenly in its lap.

Wolf got me out. He got me by the arm and pulled and led me crawling to where the Girl was. As we went I found a ring out of the Toroid under my hand. I looked at it, muzzily considered its complex beauty and put it in a side pouch.

"What . . . what happened?" The Girl was shaken too. Her helmet had a great scar on it and she'd been well dusted with rust.

"Get out," I said. "We've got to get away from here . . ." The lights flicked and then came on again before she could panic.

"Did you get the Toroid?"

"It blew . . . everything blew!" I led limping up the corridor. We had to get away from there, I had to tell the Fat Man about the Matter Engine before it was too late.

"You didn't get the Toroid?"

"Only a part . . . but I have it all . . . all in my head."

We rounded the last of the lead shields, entered the Deep

Machine. I tasted the radiations there and it was dying too. The power, I thought, the power. When I'd cut the Matter Engine I'd cut off the power, it'd all die now, it was only a matter of time. The Machine would die with all its structures and the people could live again, they'd have a struggle sure, but that was what they needed. The nutrient would flow for a while, it might take the Machine a decade to really finish, it'd be a gradual let down and the people would survive.

As I went past the master place I jerked down the screen and broke the circuits there. It wasn't necessary, but I made sure just the same. We ran through the dimming lights, the diminishing images of the Machine. Wolf found where the tunnel was and we went out that way.

CHAPTER SIXTEEN

THE TUNNEL DIDN'T compress to try me this time. Those mechanisms were finished with, that was all past. I doubt the Machine was aware of us any more, it certainly didn't bother now that it was dying. I thought how maybe I was dying too, I'd taken a load of radiation, looking too long into the Matter Engine. Alarm signals were bleating all over my body.

Anyway, I didn't know how long I'd go on now my Purpose was done. I wasn't even sure how much I was part of the Deep Machine, it was possible I'd just end slowly with it. But I still had to last long enough to make it to the Fat Man and give him the design for the Matter Engine, the shape of the Toroids. I had to put that into his hands so that the Corps could survive, so that the man race wouldn't all go like on the Streets. It was my new Purpose and as important as the last one.

I landed rolling on the floor of the Control Room. They were still yelling and celebrating their imaginary Rocket. The party wasn't over yet. When I got up Wolf had his ears back and was looking quickly left and right from the tunnel to where the soldiers still had the Girl.

The Boy—it had to be the Boy, playing the same old game—he came bundling out the way I'd come. I moved quickly and pointed my pistol at him. If I'd known who it was he wouldn't have got behind me and I'd have been a lot more worried back there.

"You *Android*!" The Girl started to struggle again. She clawed at the soldiers arms, bit their fingers.

"No good!" The Boy's voice was still muffled through his helmet but when I heard him I wondered how I could ever have been fooled. "The Engine's burst . . ." He laughed, looking at my face. Then he turned back to his sister. "He couldn't have moved it anyway, he got a ring out of it though." Then he pulled a toggle on the front of his suit and cleanser fizzed out and covered him. He couldn't see then so I did the same thing for myself and Wolf. We stood there, cloaked in columns of foam, trying to watch each other.

"You didn't kill him," said the Girl. I couldn't tell if she was sorry. The Boy shook his foam off and unclipped the collars of his helmet. Then he took it and threw it at me.

"I near to got him in there. I can't kill him now, but I nearly got him in there. I thought I could get the Toroid myself until I saw it . . ."

"Then you won't get your medal," sneered the Girl. She struggled some more, got a hand free and beat at the soldiers. "Let me *go*!" They didn't even flinch when she scratched their eyes. They weren't very elaborate Androids. Not even as bright as Wolf, they were soldiers.

"That what *you* wanted, sis? A medal was it? Let those soldiers go! Let them alone! A medal and having it off with *that*? Your dirty old Candy Man! That and anything else—let the Androids go!"

"Research! A scientist must research!" She went quiet and smiled to herself. She knew she'd got to the Boy about his medals. "I got some good things in the mountain palaces. You shan't have any!"

"I'm going!" The Boy spun and took two quick paces away. "I'm leaving here!" He came back and grinned at

148

me. "You relax, Candy, yes, you *relax*. I won't kill you after all. I won't even try until after you've told us all about the Matter Engines." His face went serious. "You wouldn't like to tell *me*? You wouldn't like me to take it all down?"

I believe he meant it and, for a moment, I considered it. Better to tell him than have it all lost if I ended.

The Girl screamed with rage. Kicked again and again in the soldiers' arms. One of the bright helmets fell and bounced on the floor.

"I wouldn't kill you at all then, I'd let you go on." The Boy was all smiles. "I don't want the ring, you could keep that bit of Toroid . . . ?"

"He will! He hates you!" She got her legs free for a moment but they soon had her again. I grinned. I'd done my Purpose, I didn't care if I lived or died just so long as the Corps got the Engine, and I knew the Boy wouldn't kill me until I passed the information.

Nobody said anything. We stood in the noise of the party while I pretended to consider. I wouldn't have told the Boy the time by the clock on his own wall. Anyway, he couldn't have held it all in his head like me. Even the Fat Man would need a pretty good computer to understand it. That party was getting louder and louder. One of the technicians came and urinated behind a console near us. We still stood there, I enjoyed keeping them waiting.

"You couldn't take it down," I said at last. "There aren't the words to speak it, not even the numbers. It's a thing that must be between Machines." Men, they were just left behind by what they'd invented, they didn't have the chance to understand what they were doing, that was part of their trouble. "The Engine is too much for *explanation*. Perhaps I could give you a sonnet, an *image* for it. I could express it for you . . ."

"All right!" The Boy cut right across me. He picked up his helmet from where it had fallen, looked at it like it was a strange thing and threw it at my head again. I only just got under that time, maybe my reflexes had started to go already. "You're dead, Candy! If nothing else does,

I'll get you!" He stormed off up the steps and on to the balcony.

"Come on!" I said to the Girl. I nodded to the soldiers and they set her gently on to the ground. They came to attention, presented arms and stood at ease. As far as I know they're still there.

"You coming, K?" It was the first time I'd called her by name since what happened at that Cottage. There was a pang remembering, even then, for a second I wished I was a man. But then I thought how I wouldn't even have had a Purpose, how I'd have been long dead anyway.

"Yes, Candy . . ." She'd noticed it too. She was calm now, a little sad I thought. Maybe I saw regret in her eyes, but how can you tell what people really think? She waited a moment and when she spoke again her voice was fierce. "You, I'm not letting you out of my sight. You're all we've got now. I'm not letting him near you, we can't lose now."

We went threading through the party and towards the door. Wolf pattered at our heels. One thing, those people were feeling good. That girl that took her glasses off, she was dancing bare chested now and it seemed to excite them all. Men, they never seemed to see the woods for the trees, to know what parts were really important.

"Very funny!" said the Girl when I put it to her. Then she asked how I could joke at a time when things were so serious. I just said that I wasn't joking.

We went right through there and nobody noticed except someone said how the soldier statues seemed to have come to life. Then he shook his head and said it was impossible and to forget it.

In the open I took Wolf in my arms and we set off on the fly-belts across the Rocket Plain. Maybe my belt had lost power in the radiations—the dog's weight didn't help either—so we couldn't gain height very quickly. We took two miles and five minutes to get to just fifty feet.

As we threaded out through the Rockets I could see the Boy far over to the left, hovering amongst the nose cones as he followed us.

"You really did it?" The Girl had been looking back and I turned too. It didn't look much back there, there

150

wasn't any sign that anything important had happened. The lights were still on and the music was as loud as ever.

"It'll take a while," I told her. "It'll take a while to run through the programmes, it'll take years to get through the music sequences."

"What'll it be like? I mean . . . a world without the lights, all the layers dark, without the calming illusions, without music. Without the Machines or the Teachers to care for the people. There won't even be any nutrient, it'll be hell!"

"It'll be all right. They'll learn to look after themselves again."

"How can they?" I didn't know the answer to that, so I said nothing. I wished I could be there to help. "You know it'll be *hell*!"

We just had to get back quickly with the information to the Fat Man. That was the only thing now. The Corps had to have the power to expand the race to the galaxies, to put the world to rights, or to shift the population to new worlds.

"*Some* will survive . . ." said the Girl. She licked her lips. "It might be a good thing for them. Thin the weakest out. Civilisation needs an occasional excursion into barbarity. It'll be fun to watch. I could do some observations, write a paper."

We lifted out over the parcel wall, moved on over the raft and towards the Streets and pillars. You could smell the smoke from where the Teachers had pulverised that Buddha. When we got there they were sitting in their chairs and doing nothing. They looked up as we passed and I saw one move his hands on his keyboard, but they got nothing back from the Machine and they hardly seemed to notice us. Looking down you could see gobbets of plastic burning, it was as if we were right over their heads.

The Boy still followed us. Once when we stopped to rest my arms from carrying Wolf we heard his belt buzzing far up in the beams. I saw him for a moment, moving up there in the shadows. Then we set out and crossed that dark ocean, came out on the other side in almost the place we'd come from. This time we didn't bother with the valleys. We hovered up those low cliffs, up that wall face of broken rooms and struck directly inland.

Another hour and the Girl had taken us to a Cottage. This time it was right up under a Street and in another clump of long dead trees. My dark vision seemed weaker after the Matter Engine so I had to rely on the Girl's light. We landed in the crumbling sticks and walked to the door in the small shining of her toothpick. I saw my own hands were glowing radiation and further away there were some lights. You could see the Streets march away over the smooth, dead hills.

"It's OK to use these places now," said the Girl. "I don't think the Teachers will interfere. They won't do anything without the Machine."

When we got the door open the Cottage was just the same as all the others. The Girl didn't open the console right away, she went to a locker and got fresh clothes out of it. Feminine stuff, like she wore when we were together. She shucked off her rubbers and stood to look at me for a moment.

I couldn't stand to watch that, so I went away to the back of the Cottage. The light was too hard for me too, so I got out that old bandage of mine and wrapped it over my eyes. I'd had a headache since the Engine and now it was getting worse, maybe it was being near the Girl, but I didn't think so. Anyway, that old familiar half world I saw through the fabric was safe and I felt a little better.

"You look bad, Candy." I heard her clothes rustle, but I didn't look, it hurt too much to turn my head. "You could die you know . . ." The cloth still rustled. "You wouldn't like to tell me about the Engine—give me that ring? Just to be safe?"

I didn't answer. I considered it, pretended not to hear. Then I ran through the Engines in my head, fixed them there again, made sure I could hold it all. I couldn't give her that ring, it was still too hot, its radiations could kill any human dead.

"You loved me once, I'm not like my brother. You could trust me. There might even be a chance of repairing you."

I still didn't say anything. There was some broken pottery and a hammer lying on the table back there. I pretended to go through the shards, holding them up to see, raking them through my fingers.

"Candy . . . ?"

"It doesn't matter," I said. "I'll end when the time comes." All I had to do was remember long enough, just as long as I kept thinking about it it'd be all right.

"You think you'd get a better deal from the Fat Man? I doubt it. I could protect you from my brother . . ."

"It's not that." I found a shard that didn't fit with the others. I wondered what the pots would look like if they were the perfect shape that Potter was trying for, I wondered where the odd fragment came from. It was made of plaster for one thing, the edges smooth and regular, with triangular, pyramid, notches on one side and similar projections on the other. It was different from the others, alone like me, a part of something, but still not like the rest.

"Candy? You all right?"

"Yes. I couldn't tell you. I need a computer to tell, a Deep Machine. You can't explain it . . ."

"All right . . . take it easy, Candy, save yourself." She came to me then and took my arm. "Your eyes going? I'd do something for you, but I don't know how." She sounded sorry for me, but I still thought that she could be acting. I stood and waited and the Girl went to the console. I found that bit of plaster in my hand so I dropped it into my pouch and by that time the lights had blinked and the Cottage had wavered and we were at where we were going.

When we went out of the other door we stepped into the metal corridor again. My legs shook as we went up there and when the Fat Man opened a door for us I couldn't see who it was. I went from wall to wall like a drunk man.

"Free fall," said the Girl. "The artificial gravity is minimal." Maybe it was too, but by the time we reached the couch room I was glad enough to lie on the slab. It was nearer the end, that much on. I could almost feel my cells dying. I just hoped I could remember everything.

The Fat Man adjusted me on the slab. They fitted the

plugs and leads to my body. While the Girl fed me tubes the Man checked dials over there.

"A bad, bad state." I felt a little better for the tubes but when the Fat Man came towards me he was shaking his head. "In a bad condition . . ."

"Hurry . . ." My voice sounded strange to me. "Quick, while I can hold on to it . . ."

They didn't have to give me my codes or stimulation that time. The Fat Man just said he was ready and I gave it all out. Some of it was words, but mostly it was between me and the Ship's Deep Machine. I could feel my concentration slipping sometimes, it was a hard thing, it took all my strength.

"You're sure the Matter Engine was destroyed?" It was the last thing the Fat Man asked me.

"Sure . . . quite sure . . ." I was sure all right. There was something else I knew I should tell him too, I knew that. But I was really ill right then, the mists were coming in, I couldn't think of what to say. The effort of holding it all in my head was getting too much. Soon I'd have to find somewhere quiet or it'd all go. I'd forgotten I'd told the Fat Man and it didn't matter any more.

"No hope?" said the Fat Man.

"He's going," I heard the Girl say.

"I meant the Matter Engine . . . the Toroid." The Fat Man glanced down into my face.

"Maybe I've already told you," I heard myself say. "Maybe I told you yesterday . . . perhaps it doesn't even matter . . ."

They went away then. The Fat Man went to a row of screens across the room and started checking what the Ship was making of the information I'd given it. I was glad just to lie there, I didn't even mind looking at the Girl. She got interested in the flashing lights and patterns over there and joined the Fat Man. I watched their silhouettes against the colour coded models the Ship projected. The Fat Man moved close to her and they were talking together in low voices. The lights gleamed and glinted like diamonds and rubies, emeralds and sapphires too, amethysts . . . It was beautiful.

I couldn't stand it any more. Maybe it was the Girl

leaving me like that, or perhaps it was the bright lights, all that clicking and whirring. I couldn't take it. Suddenly I had to get off to be somewhere secret, alone and preferably in the dark.

I drove my thick fingers to get a handful of tubes. I dropped most of them but I managed to give myself half a dozen one after the other. A while later I felt a little better and swung my legs off the slab. I took off the transfers and leads and made it towards the door. They didn't even look up to see me go.

Through the door the steel passage went left to the Cottage and right to somewhere else, so I turned right. I didn't want any more of Cottages or the world beyond them. I scraped and slithered, half walked away from there. Then I noticed a curious clicking behind me. I managed to get my pistol out and it was poor old Wolf. He wasn't as bad as me, but he was looking pretty old. It was OK though, he was all right, he'd get better, I knew it when I tried his handle. I was glad to see him.

CHAPTER SEVENTEEN

WOLF LED and I followed up that slow endless corridor. The walls were polished metal, the ceiling and floors were matt black. Whenever I got my head up to look, a million Candy Makers reflected away on either side. We all looked terrible.

We got to the end; the floor stopped and I fell off it. I dragged myself up and we were in this vast room that had no roof except the stars.

I stopped to take it in. It was a while before I was sure what I was seeing. The floor was black like the corridor, but it was shining now. Mirror polished and black with the intensity of space, a quality of shining velvet, all studded with the uncountable stars, perfectly flat, like the calm of ancient water. I looked down and saw my ravaged face reflected all crowned and framed with the heavens. There were no walls that I could see, no roof at all, the stars repeated above, remote and close, somehow too beautiful.

The Moon was there. That old cratered thing hung heavy and half full, shadow side lit a little by star-shine and Earth-glow. It was clear out there, as clear as my head used to be when I'd had a good tube. The Moon looked too big, after a struggle I measured it and we were half-way there.

When I turned the Earth was on the other side, low down over the corridor blister. Like the Moon, the lit side was down. The squared off oceans were twinned below on the shining floor, it was like being in space without even a suit between you and the cosmos. I felt weak, unprotected. I wondered what mattered, why we didn't just go away and forget everything.

On the star-jewelled floor lay silent instruments, array upon array of antennae spindled thin against the sky, etched black, involved patterns across the sunlit Earth. Small coloured pinpoints of light winked from consoles, thick transfers and cables came up out of the floor, divided and dividing again as they reached into the instruments. There were even some small optical telescopes, set about with tables and deck chairs, for men, I supposed. There were small fences of luminous metal around each complex so that the antennae were lit from beneath as well as from the sky.

But I didn't take any of that in, not at first. What I was looking at were the great uncouth lumps of stone which ringed through the delicacy of the machines.

All were ten, maybe fifteen feet high, mostly capped with great lintels as thick as themselves. The innermost circle was tight packed, the outer more spread out, it was all concentric with the gallery itself.

Some of the stones were laid down, mostly they were still encased with that same plastic stuff as the Buddha, some of them were raised up on cubes of clear glassy material, to make up for the ground they'd stood on, I suppose.

Eerie. It was eerie in that combined Earth and Moon-light. It was *magic* there, a magic light, the light of time and space and vastness. Blue and cool and the stones deep

156

and dark in their shadows, occluding against those infinite stars. It was strong, too strong for me, stronger than men, more powerful than all the doings of life, than all the Moonlit gossamer of the instruments, the dark underbrush of subtle telescopes and sensors.

It saddened me. All that eternity and me ending. I'd never felt like that, not in my two thousand years, but I'd never been ill before and this was the first time I'd contemplated my Purpose. I felt maudlin, I looked at the stars and I'd have cried if I could.

I took myself towards the great double ring of standing stones. When I walked into one I half collapsed into the shadows under it. Wolf curled up and grunted at my feet, someone had cut an axe shape, double edged, into it. I put my hand there. Vandals, I thought, men spoiling everything. It had all been spoiled, everything, it was a good place to end in. I felt really bad.

I never slept before, but I think I did then. When the voices started I still lay there. I don't know when I first heard them, but when I recognised the Boy I woke up in a hurry. I felt a bit better then, sharp enough anyway to pull my legs into the shadow and lie still. I touched my cheek and it was scraped where it had slid down the stone.

"Look, a stepped pyramid . . . any of mine you like . . . just for one sarsen! Any of these . . . any stone!"

The Boy slapped a stone a few feet from where I was. I got Wolf's handle and hoped he'd be quiet. I couldn't face the Boy then. I had to go on again too, somehow in my confusion I'd remembered that segment of Toroid that I had and something else I had to do too. I wasn't going to let that Boy have the Toroid—not by killing me. Anyhow, in a way I was worried, in my weakness you could have called it fear.

"Look here!" It was the Potter talking. He sounded a little angry. "You've got your Junter Munter! What d'you want Stonehenge for? Give your pyramids to the public collection. That's what I'll do with the Henge."

"It's OK for you old ones, in at the start. Anyway the Junter Munter is on level one—it's not got half its value down there. Come on! Just one stone?"

"Astronomy. D'you know, that's what they were for. All of them. No. Not one stone, it's a set."

"I can't stand here all day. I want to kill that Android before he dies. Get him preserved. He's a wonderful messo-space Artifact!"

"Doesn't the Moon look good shining through the stones? Look at the stars! Think . . . if there are infinite stars, why isn't there total, universal starlight? D'you see?"

"Don't put me off, Potter! What about it, anyway? What about my stones?"

"It's a little . . . a little *dirty*. D'you know? All this commerce in dead man's things that should be buried with them. Not decent to kill Candy Man just to stuff him. He's conscious—like it or not, even if he wasn't intended—he's practically human. It's be wrong to do it to a man, d'you see?"

"A *Corps* Man!" The Boy laughed out loud. *"That'd* be wrong! But you can't treat things like him as human! You can't treat any of those things from the Streets like men . . ."

"I heard your sister does."

The Boy went silent for a moment. When he spoke again it was very quietly, his voice was full of anger.

"That was experimental, scientific. Anything's all right if you're only trying it. Anyway, he'll pay—he's going to get stuffed!"

"I heard you tried to kill him before."

"He's not so good now. I was waiting, just *waiting*. For the Toroid. I'll get him this time . . ." There was another silence before the Boy went on. "The Taj Mahal, I'll give you that other pinnacle. I'll give you a brand new V8, a perfect 1938 V8 Ford? What about it? I'll divide . . . I'll take half a stone . . . ?"

"I said I don't like this *commerce*. This dealing in Artifacts, they're *sacred*, they mean something. Men made them for *reasons*. They're important to trade in. Those old men that made them, what would they think, d'you know?"

"Glad someone cared still. Come on! What will you take?"

158

"The Artifacts ought to be in a public collection. They belong to everybody."

"That's stupid! Everything belongs to who can pay! Things belong to who can get them."

"It's too important to you. A lust! Like your sister and . . ."

"Leave her out! I'm going. I need to kill that Candy!"

"That Android, he's had a bad deal. He should be given treatment. He only did what he was supposed to do!" The Potter's voice was slowly rising. When he finished he was nearly shouting. "Wrong to kill him just to mount him on a wall!"

"I'll come back!" The Boy was shouting too. He started to walk away. "I won't go without a stone!"

"What he really wants is the altar." The Potter was speaking normally now, talking to himself as the Boy went away. "All the thought of that ancient blood to gloat over, he'd like that!" He sighed, I heard him start to come towards me. "There's only the one thing I want. He wouldn't even see it unless there was blood on it . . ."

I rolled and managed to look out at him. There was no one else there. I needed help badly. Maybe the Potter seemed sympathetic, I thought maybe he'd help me. Anyway, I had nothing to lose. I waited for him to come towards me.

"Only a perfect shape . . ." He chuckled to himself, the moonlight struck his white hair. "I'm not even sure I knew what it meant . . ."

"Mr. Potter . . ." I tried to roll more into the light.

"I've had it . . . I had it once . . ." He was looking down as he walked, shaking his head to himself. "Now, if he could find that again for me . . ."

I got my back against one stone and started to push myself up. I managed to speak again. "Help me . . ."

"Who's there?" He stopped, stared up into my face. "It's you . . ." He didn't seem surprised or frightened. He just came and helped me up. "Y'know that Boy wants you hung on his wall? He's not right in the head."

"I need help . . ."

"Yes. They did bad by you, Android. You did your best for them."

"I got a part of the Engine. I was ill . . . I forgot . . . I didn't tell them . . ." I fished that shining thing out of my rubbers, held it out to him. The lights twinkled and flashed in our faces, made strange patterns on the stones. He didn't seem to care about it, maybe he didn't realise how significant it was. "It's from the Matter Engine, give you all the power you need . . ."

"It's a delusion . . . But what's *this*?" Somehow I had that fragment of plaster out too. When I gave him the Toroid I put that into his hand as well. I couldn't feel it, I didn't have control over things like that any more, there was no sensation in either of my hands. When he held it up I remembered getting it in the Cottage.

"It's mine!" The Potter held it up to the light of the ring and looked at it. "D'you know, this is it!"

"Something I found in a Cottage—what about the Toroid?"

"Yes, a good shape, it was the *one*! I made a mould. This was the last piece . . ." He was smiling to himself, he held the plaster so he hardly touched it. "How could I have lost it?"

"Will you take care of the Toroid? See they make new Engines?"

"The ring . . . ?" He took a brief look at it and dropped it in his pocket. Then he went on fondling the plaster. He was as mad as the Boy, he'd forgotten what was important. It was crazy to think about there being a perfect shape, he didn't say what it was perfect for. He was as mad as the Boy.

"Look . . ." I made a last effort. "I don't think I can finish this, please see to it. That's a part of the big Toroid on the *Matter Engine* . . ." He didn't seem to realise what I was talking about.

"I can make more now. Slip-mould them, all in the good old way, produce them . . . a hundred thousand. A million perfect shapes, fill the world with them . . ." He was away and dreaming. Aesthetics were like sex to the Girl for him. I almost gave up, just waited there, watching him with my dimming eyes.

"Please . . ."

"Thank you, Candy Man, you don't know how important this is, a world of perfect shapes . . . think what a difference that'll make! The race can end on a note of perfection . . ." Sure, I thought, they were *advanced*, I was only an outdated Android from too long ago and dying on my feet. How could I expect to have their values, to understand them? How could they have the same urgencies as myself? How could they care if I died?

But then I thought how they'd made me. How I was like them really, in their image. They owed me a lot for that. It was their fault I existed, that I was in this trouble, they made me, they should have cared. A small anger grew in me. If I'd had the strength I'd have picked him up and shaken him.

"Ah . . . Candy Man . . ." He put the mould carefully away. "Time for that. I'll bury the pots for archaeologists, they'll be something good to remember this age for. Someone has to think about the Artifacts of now . . ." He looked up at me. "God . . . but you look bad! Sloppy . . . you look sloppy and drunk!"

"Radiation . . . everything's shot . . ."

"A slow thing, a slow consumption, I suppose, killing you by degrees . . . ?"

"That doesn't matter. It couldn't matter less. The Matter Engines—send the Corps to the galaxies, start again, you'll have the power . . ."

"Magnetism, would y'say? Radiation overload, perhaps we can do something about that." I told him again how it didn't matter. It didn't really, but I was weakened and I was human enough to weaken more and want to live, or maybe it was just easier to agree with him, let him lead me to the inner stones. I listened to Wolf click behind and tried to keep not caring. It'd have been hell if I'd started to fear. I was far gone, I don't know what I was thinking.

"Yes . . . we've got equipment . . ." The Potter walked across the inner ring and stopped by a horizontal stone there. He took my arm and put me to lie on my back. I was still telling him how it didn't matter and how when I died everything would solve itself. He didn't hear, maybe my articulation was gone too far.

"An astronomical thing, y'know, they say they used to make human sacrifices here. That's what the Boy wants it

161

for. Now . . ." he came back to my troubles, "we'll just put you through the correction program for the telescopes. Ship'll take care of it . . . the Ship's Deep Engine. Don't worry, it'll be like the other times . . ."

He disappeared and left me to lie trying to count stars. Then he was back again, wheeling some sort of shiny trolley. I didn't have strength to argue more. I just lay and let him make the connections. I went spinning down that darkening, terrible Street of memories, it soon went blank.

The next thing was that there was this searching in my head and I was somewhere else. My legs jerked experimentally, my fingers did things on their own. It was strange having my body checked out by something else, every muscle got exercised. The Ship was different from the other Deep Engine, but just as potent . . . it was odd, the Ship was un-me and I wasn't a part of it. When my head was turned that way I got glimpses of the Potter's face over the patterned lights on the trolley.

For a long time I felt the tweaking of currents and signals, the sensations as the modulations flowed through me. The whole thing went further and deeper than anything I'd had before, it seemed to take for ever. Then my feet tingled and I could move my toes again, my thought and vision began to clear, I found that I could see infra-red and the other way too when I screwed my eyes. I began to feel good again and I was glad about it.

The sun came up over the edge of the Gallery as the Ship turned. The cupola suddenly flashed white and then turned to amber and blood red as the filters came on. I felt the last series of checks, when I opened my eyes my head was facing the sun and I saw it rise through the frame of great stones. It was warm to me. I could feel everything, I saw the forest of antennae light up like gold.

I tried to sit up, but the Ship wouldn't let me. There was something else yet.

"Feeling better?" The Potter put away his piece of plaster, I hadn't seen him take it out. He came across to me, I heard him but I couldn't answer. "It was the magnetism. The Ship says you will need adjustment in thirty-six hours, it's done the best it can, the treatment may not be effective in the long run."

162

I didn't care about that. I was feeling strong again. Strong enough to take the Boy, to face the Girl, strong enough to carry the World a little longer. I switched my eyes about and they lit on that spare pistol sticking out of my opened rubbers.

"And there's something else," said the Potter. "The Ship went right through you. Deeper than ever before. Maybe the World Deep Engine knew and didn't tell you, but the Ship found out." I tried to get up but I wasn't allowed to. I began to wonder what was the matter, what had gone wrong.

"Brace yourself!" said the Potter—and then the Ship told me. It spoke directly into my mind and told me that I wasn't an Android. Not really . . . that really I was a man.

I didn't want to move any more. I just lay there, staring at the greasy, black butt of the pistol.

CHAPTER EIGHTEEN

IT WAS LIKE being hit with a hammer. I lay still, if I'd been free I wouldn't have moved. They'd just cut the world out under me again, it'd all gone upside down.

I got my eyes off the gun and looked at the Potter. He was bent over the service trolley, his eyes bright in the lights there as he studied his little piece of mould. Hope came to me, crazy hope, like all the humans have.

Somehow it was right being a man, as if I'd known it all my life. It was the *hope* of it, you don't have much to hope for if you're an Android, you just go on doing your Purpose, it's only men have crazy hope. I hadn't realised I'd hated being an Android.

"I don't eat . . . the *tubes* . . . I can drink nerve gas . . ." It was suddenly ridiculous, stupid, more illusions, more layers on another surface of lies. I was thinking of the Girl, dreaming sweet dreams of K. I didn't dare hope.

"*Remember everything,*" said the Ship in my head. "*We*

163

remember everything, we are deeper than anything built before us on Earth or off it. We hold the patterns, all the knowledge Machines ever had, we made ourselves to take it all to the stars. We had your number, Candy Man. We knew you all the time."

I still didn't want to move. My legs trembled, I didn't dare believe it, I still couldn't quite accept it even though it was so right.

"Remember what the Fat Man told you. Concerning the Star Ships. How men travelled deep space."

"Y'know you thought you had it both ways?" The Potter had started talking as well. "Thought you could have the powers of a Machine and the conscious of a man, have your cake and eat it, d'you know?" The Ship ignored him and so did I.

"Men could not survive 'time'," the Ship went on. "There had to be methods. Far in history we tried varied things. Sorts of hibernation and suspension on the cold treks. Slowed heart beats, coupled slow machines for hearts and kidneys, brains separate and pickled in nutrients, brittle storage at near absolute zero. We tried things. We moved whole populations living and breeding. Men and women, living their history along the star ways, breeding was not true in those conditions, the stresses of high light fractions. Distortions, an imperceptible changing by generations, the becoming something else, something worse. Ending in inbred hells of monsters—all the proud, gigantic Ships; in the end the people died.

"So we made alternate things, long eons of ideas." The Ship seemed to pull itself together, to come back to the present. *"We made the Ship/Rider mechanism, and so the Corps made the first great crossing. Traversed the Galaxy and found it empty—but that is another story. The mechanism dissolves men and women. Brings their bodies and minds to charge and counter charge, to yes or no a billion times on our deep tapes and records. Dissolved to component atoms, to tiny reactions recorded as patterns in our deep spools, so that they would last as long as ourselves. As long as we self-perpetuating Ships. So that we would remember them for ever. Small notations—we can*

*write a man in fourteen and one half metres of a record
wire, all to be reconstituted as required . . .*

"*Perhaps it could be said that all we Deep Machines
are partly human, a sort of marriage. Men all the time
contributing to us—to our reality . . .*" The Ship was off
again, dreaming. I was fascinated, trying to fit it all to
what I knew of myself, but I wished the Ship would stick
to the point. Over by the trolley I'll swear the Potter was
singing to his bit of mould. In a way the Ship was as bad
as him. It just went on and on talking. "*A revelation for
us . . . a dawn of new things. A Renaissance . . . a vast
extension of our perceptions . . . all the minds of entire
races.*"

"What about me?" Maybe I was shouting, it certainly
felt like it.

"*You? You were made from a man. By that mechanism.
When you were a man the Earth's Deep Machine took your
patterns and made them a part of itself, then it remade you
an Android. You know what you were made to do. You
volunteered, you were made a machine to last. Your mind
is a man's but with certain enhancements and adaptions.
Connections, facilities from the Deep Machine . . .*"

"What now?" I always knew. I told you how I always
knew. Hope opened out again and it didn't seem so crazy
now. I basked in speculations of future glory. I was a *man.*
There was more in my existence than what I was meant to
do. I could be part of the Corps, I could span the galaxies
and have the Girl, I could be anything I thought about!
I was a member of the human race—right *then,* on that
new crest of reaching out, the heat of the Renaissance the
Matter Engines would bring. I'd be one of the super beings
I'd made possible!

"What now?" I said more quietly.

"*We can make a man of you. We can put you back to
flesh and breathing . . .*"

"Well—do it!" I mean, what else? It was like a birth-
day for me, I could hardly wait. I remembered then how
they'd slapped my back when I'd volunteered, how they'd
wished me Luck.

"*Think!*" said the Ship. "*You just think about it.*"

There were disadvantages. I'd be more vulnerable. I'd

be fragile if I ever met the Boy again. A snake could kill me, a bee maybe.

"*You're immortal now,*" said the Ship. "*As a man you can only count on another two hundred years. You'll lose all the power and assistance of the Deep Machine—what there's left of it—and all the help we could give you . . .*"

"I never noticed much help. Make me over!"

"*Think. You're almost of us. You can detach yourself from all the race's blood and history. The ages of guilt. The things they do. You have the innocence of a Machine. Will you turn your back on that?*"

I thought about it. But what I wanted was to be a man. To take those chances, tread that glorious balance above the mud and filth. There was hope. The hope that came from the Matter Engines, that hope the small bright Toroid ring stood for. I wanted to be part of the new growth.

I looked around the antennae, the shiny perfection sun gilded by that morning, the light rays striking through the dust motes above and through the great stones, it was all there. It was beautiful and it was hopeful and profound. It was *Spring,* the Spring of my spirit and of the race. Re-birth, the race's hope and second coming. It was going to be a good time.

And the Girl. I'd almost forgotten. I hardly dared to think of her, all those things she said—perhaps she was a great whore—but she was *young.* Her mind anyway, perhaps I could get her away from her brother . . .

"*Vulnerable,*" said the Ship. "*Vulnerable to K too.*"

"That's all right!" I was shouting again. "I'll risk that . . . I don't mind . . ."

"*We can't understand. You are thinking like a man. Why be afraid of the Boy and not the Girl?*"

"That's why I must be a man. Re-make me!"

There was a long silence.

"*Unfamiliar,*" said the Ship. "*A long time since a man has been made. Not since we came out of velocity.*"

"Get on!"

"*Here? Now?*"

"Do it!"

"*You understand that you must lose your conscious? We must have the exact patterns of you now. You must*

166

cease as an Android. We hold the design, but only you have the exact patterns of now."

"Yes! Do it!" My hands were shaking and my voice was shouting.

"You will still need accompaniments. Enhancements, amplifications without which you would not be complete."

"Get on!" It was hell, the waiting. I was shaking all over.

"The foregoing is a gross over-simplification. You may not like being a man. Do you wish to go on, do you wish more information?"

"YES! NO! GET ON!"

"You must still finish your Purpose . . ."

"Of course!"

"Those capabilities—we will add what you need."

"Please . . ." I thought my head would burst. I never knew Machines could take so long.

"Shall we? Are you sure?"

"YES!" Another eternity of silence passed.

"Begin counting."

I tried to stop trembling and did that. Before I got to five I snuffed out.

I just went. Everything faded and then suddenly lights exploded and the lingering pain of my body disappeared.

There was a moment of rushing power, of cheeping sounds and lights twinkling in some secret pattern of total freedom and vast places. There was a lustrous space—and suddenly I had a body again.

"Dead . . . !" I woke and the Potter's voice was lingering in my ears from somewhere far away. When I managed to lift my lids he wasn't anywhere around.

It was a case. I was in a case with warm, thick liquids washing round me. When they sank away soft warm air struck cold as it dried me and fixed my skin.

"Do not touch anything! You will stick to it!" The Ship's voice sounded clipped and unnatural in my new ears. The Machine was speaking to me now, it didn't work directly with my brain any more, I was hearing it in the air. I looked at my hands, the whorled finger ends, it was strange to see them without the gloves. I waited, feeling my hardening parts.

167

There was a whole row of the cases, mine was the end one. Nothing moved anywhere. The room was pure white except the opaque green cases. The lights began to get brighter and I found that I could stand it. I still felt soft, I knew my skin would burst and I'd break if I fell down. I waited, getting used to it all.

Then the Ship said I was ready. I staggered out of the case and fell on my knees, on to my weak human knees. My arms were puny when I leaned forward on them, there was a feeble pad of stomach hanging under my ribs. I thought of K and started to heave myself up, I froze. There was something on my back.

I felt the weight there and horror dawned on me. Maybe I was deformed! Maybe that was why I'd volunteered to be an Android in the first place! Maybe I wasn't perfect for K and she'd turn away! Maybe they wouldn't even have me in the Corps! I twisted and glimpsed it there, pink and shiny over my white shoulder.

"You will harden," said the Ship. *"You will get a little stronger."* I remembered then, I remembered what the Ship had said to me, about the assistance and amplification I still needed from the Deep Machine. *"Remember how vulnerable you are, that you cannot carry great weights."* It was true enough, but I just swore and staggered and went weaving off to find a way out.

"Remember you will tire!" There were small speakers set all the way beside me. That thing across my shoulders was heavy. I could feel it vibrate as it worked there and I didn't like it much. I wished the Ship would stop telling me how weak I was, I knew that already.

I stopped trying to run and concentrated on getting my body to behave itself. My legs felt too long and too heavy, I had to spread them to stand properly. I stood a moment, my head down, screwing up my face and trying to stop the tingling. It didn't seem all that good being a man, it ought to have been better. I wondered if I ought to have a new name now, I wondered what I looked like and then I couldn't get the question out of my head. I didn't think I could be as ugly as I felt, all soft and too big for my strength, with a head like a melon. The light kept getting better but there weren't any mirrors.

"You're ready . . ." said the little speakers. The wall at the end opened up for me and I went that way.

It was the same. The room just became a corridor. Still brilliant matt white, still no reflections. It was eight sided and I realised that it was the core of the Ship. The central passage where the Deep Machines were best protected. All around would be great chambers that contained the driving parts. In places the walls were dulled, the grey condensation there showed where the cold behind there had come through. I knew there'd be only one way out—right up at the far end, to where the Gallery was, to where I'd left the Potter. The corridor seemed to curve up and then down that way, but that was just the forces in the driving parts affecting light. I padded on the way I had to go.

There were some sets of rubbers hanging on the wall. I took a set and stretched on the lower part. The top wouldn't go on because of the thing on my back, but I still felt better, more protected. There were pistols there too, so I hung one on my waistband, put the rope around my neck. I felt really like a man then. There weren't any gloves, but I had begun to feel I might not need them.

Half a mile down the corridor a star pattern of ladders wound down from slots in the walls and floors. There were lenses set there too, I could tell that they were watching me. I put my hands on to the ladder that seemed to lead up. When I didn't get a shock or anything I began to climb.

It was rough up that slot. Cold too. The heating and insulation were right at the minimum. Great tufts of sponge stuff had ripped out of the linings. The absolute zero you need for that kind of driving parts was hell to create in the first place, a deadly thing, you have to think of it as active, as a sort of energy and then it was worse to keep it back. It was only an inspection tunnel that I was in, it was just for access, no one was expected to like it there.

A hundred feet up I started to feel tired. I wondered if I'd always be climbing around inside things, I took great gasping breaths and the inside of my rubbers was running stinking sweat. It sure wasn't like being an Android.

The slot ended in a heavy trap door. I pushed at it and

it clicked and swung easily up as the Ship opened for me. I climbed out and I was in a proper, four sided corridor. It was as long as the Gallery, but the walls weren't reflective and neither was the floor. I still couldn't see myself.

Doors were set maybe every twenty feet up the opposite wall, so I went that way, trying them as I went. There wasn't anyone about and all the doors were locked.

I was just thinking how I might have to go back when the next door clicked before I touched it, then opened half an inch.

I flattened back against the wall and got out my pistol. I stood there and looked at the ribbon of brighter light that cut across the corridor. After a while I went and pushed the door with my gun muzzle. The door swung in silently and I stepped through. Then it shut behind me with a click so soft I hardly heard it.

It was a big room in there. Not wide, but long, up the walls there were green cases like the one I'd come out of. Their pilot lights were minimal and you could tell they were shut down. I looked beyond them to the far end. There was a ramp moving up and out of sight and I started to walk that way. Then I caught the grey gleam of mirrors. I speeded up and as I went I watched them. It was a crazy thing, me hurrying towards *mirrors* after the horror I'd had of them; but it was very important to me what I looked like and I wasn't watching anything else.

I went on down there, all the time looking to see myself come forward in the mirrors. When I was thirty yards off I saw I was just exactly the same as I ever was. I didn't have Wolf any more, only the bright orange rubber pants, my man body above with hair on it now, that great pistol on its lanyard around my neck like an albatross. I was human all right. A lot weaker, sure, different, a lot less confident, I had that thing on my back, but I looked exactly the same. I kept on going in, closer and closer, staring and not believing it, trying to see some small thing that had changed. I was so absorbed I didn't notice the sounds, or see the soft padding spread on the floor until I fell over it and sprawled on the naked legs there.

I apologised and rolled on to my back. The ceiling was hung with soft draperies, a great concave, magnifying mirror was slung beneath them. I saw that I was surrounded with mirrors, that there was a sort or arbor made of them, the spaces hung with silks and sparkling things. There were spot lights there, gold plated . . . and all around, reflected, were the Boy and K. Naked together . . . him looking at me out of their embrace, over her naked buttocks.

He laughed. K started to giggle, I could see that they were ringed with cameras and recording things on trolleys.

They rolled apart. The Girl's fat parts moved, I tried to get up but the floor padding got between my feet and I fell down again. When I looked up she was propped back on her elbows and shaking with laughter. The Boy was upon his knees beside her and holding a pistol so that I could see it. He was scowling for a while but then he laughed too.

"Look at him K! A man now . . . you can tell! You're stupid Candy!"

"Looking in the mirrors, Candy?" K was still laughing, it was wilder and wilder . . . hysterical. "Looking to see if you're handsome?"

"Mirror, mirror on the wall . . ." The Boy rubbed the pistol on his cheek. "Not you, Candy, not with that hunch back . . ."

"Did you know you were deformed, Candy Man?" She smiled at me, then started laughing again. Maybe it was the expression on my face.

I hadn't thought of him and K being like that. They were horrible, it was horrible in all those lights and mirrors. I never liked mirrors . . . never, like I never liked touching things.

"Looking at yourself, Candy? Like that do you? Candy . . . you like yourself too much!"

"He liked me," said the Girl. "I found him satisfactory. I quite liked you when you were an Android, Candy . . ."

"You sure that wasn't because you were disguised as me?" The Boy was laughing as much as her now. "You know, you're the legitimate object for his lusts. There's nothing you could put past our Candy . . ."

The Girl, I'd hoped for her. Maybe, I told myself,

maybe he'd forced her . . . maybe those long space journeys, maybe he'd corrupted her. Perhaps when she'd thought I was dead, or the horror of finding I was an Android, perhaps she didn't care any more, and then he'd got her. Maybe, I thought . . . maybe with love and care and tenderness . . . maybe I could win her back. I thought I could see tears in her eyes, I thought she might be crying, but really I knew it was from laughing.

I took it out of the Ship. I cursed it for letting all this happen, for providing mirrors and the recording trolleys, for letting there be things like that. There was a second's silence, then something clicked and the Ship answered.

"Don't blame us for what they do with us! We're innocent!" I said once more how it was a bastard, but that didn't make sense and it didn't even make me feel better.

"You take a good look at the mirrors, Candy! I said I'd kill you when you didn't expect it! Look last, Candy Man!"

Hell, this time it really mattered! My stomach turned to water and I realised how much I didn't want to die. The Girl screamed or laughed or something and I saw the Boy bringing up his pistol.

He took a step forward and fired, but he fell over on the Girl, so he missed me. I didn't know—for a moment I thought she might have tripped him—but really he just fell in the padding the way I did. Even then I was sad she hadn't tripped him.

His first charge smashed into the mirrors and brought down great dangerous chunks of glass to try and cut us up. The Girl yelped and stopped laughing.

I vaulted over the nearest of the green cases and the Boy's second shot smashed into its far side. It jerked a couple of feet towards me as I got my own pistol. Screaming alarm protests came from the Ship. Something slimy began to leak across my hands from the case. I leaned out and tried to get a clear bead on the Boy but I couldn't because the Girl was in the way. I started shooting into the padding and set it on fire.

CHAPTER NINETEEN

"STOP IT!" It was the Ship this time, shouting at us.

"I'm going to kill him! I've got to kill him!" The Boy stopped shooting the place up and started really looking for me. I saw him through a gap in the smoke, standing on one of the cases, his pistol held high as he looked about. Before I could make up my mind to shoot, the smoke curled across and I lost him. I took the chance and scuttled through the fumes to where the ramp was. When I got to it I turned to look back and let it carry me slowly up.

The Ship flushed out the smoke. The Boy was still standing there and K was on the padding pulling on her clothes. The lights on the cases suddenly came full on.

"You have got to stop it!" said the Ship. *"We will not have shooting inside us. We are regenerating the defence squad."*

"No! Wait!" The Boy jumped off the case. "No!" More lights came on like a million stars.

I saw the first cases open and the first figures come out. They looked like men, but I couldn't tell—at that moment the Boy saw me and I had to start running.

It was straight up into the Gallery. If I'd turned there somewhere I'd have made it to the Cottage maybe, but I panicked so I ended in the Gallery.

I got under that great starry dome and ran as hard as I could into the instruments. As I went a couple of charges went singing and chopping through the antennae. Smoke puffed where they struck and they made noises there like breaking springs. I just wondered how I'd had long enough to get across the open space. I ducked and ran towards Stonehenge and the Boy's charges still came smashing and tearing after me.

Ahead were the stars. They were on either side too, and behind me. They even reflected about my feet. I jinked and twisted through the undergrowth of instruments. I wondered where I thought I was going, there was only two hundred yards in any direction from where the ramp came through the floor. I stopped. I had to go back, I'd have to fight, I'd have to risk combat and make up my mind to kill the Boy if I had to. Hell, I told myself, I was human, I could do that now.

I turned, stopped and screwed my pistol to the smallest jet. I crouched through the shining instruments, looking all the time for the Boy, hunting him as he hunted me. I had to fight, there was nowhere else to go. The Henge was dark against the stars.

Over a telescope I could see the ramp blister. The Boy came running up there, then dived quickly to the left. I snapped a charge at him. He plumed a small puff of smoke and sprawled down. He tucked up his knees as if he was being born and then he died. It was as easy as that. I was surprised how easy it was to kill a man. He lay still there, just lay still.

Then it got hard again. Someone fired at me from far away to the right. At that moment the Fat Man came up the ramp. I flattened against some big dark thing and wondered what was happening. Maybe he thought he'd finished with me because when he came forward he had a pistol and it looked like he was getting ready to shoot at me. He was careless though, because he just came running straight out and I blew him down almost without trying.

I stayed low and waited. Nothing happened for a while and I took a look at where the Boy was lying. It slowly dawned on me that there was something wrong with him. That corpse had rubbers on it for a start, he'd been naked from that he was doing with the Girl when I saw him last, and he hadn't looked like dressing to kill me.

There wasn't any time to think about it. More people came up the ramp. The Boy first, then three more of him, I saw the Fat Man twice.

They all came fanning up the ramp together and they were all yelling for me. They had pistols and it was pretty clear what they meant to do. I started to shoot them down.

As they came I fired at them. I killed six before I realised some of them were Girls. I shot them down like rabbits under those cold stars, when they moved in the warm sunlight. When I'd shot K three times it didn't matter any more and I just kept on firing. There were even some cats and I shot them too.

It got me so that I shot everything that moved and I didn't even think about it. It was like a fever had me, anyway, I knew it was them or me. It was sure different from when I was an Android.

I killed them and they hardly fired at me but I had to keep moving back. Some of them made it into the thicket and began to get behind me. Then I noticed that none of them seemed to fire at me at all. When one of the Boys got close he even left his pistol on his hip and tried to get me with his bare hands. I killed him easy, it was murder. I just kept blowing them down and they kept on coming. They smashed things down, they sprawled and upset trolleys . . . my charges smashed the instruments. I ran over the thirty foot dish of an optical telepscope shouting my head off as I went. Seconds later I killed a Fat Man and he dropped his pistol and chipped the glass. All the time the Ship screamed words of rage and panic, all the time the music beat staccato and violent, the shouting punctuated by the tearing of my pistol . . . the starlight dimmed in its violent flares.

Then it all seemed to be over. I was standing there, holding out my pistol, waving it in the air to cool it. I looked at the broken and leaning antennae . . . it was a mess. I was shocked how easy it was, how little I cared. There were bodies everywhere, there were a couple of small fires that the Ship was putting out. I didn't care. I told myself they were only Androids the Ship had pulled out to protect itself. Androids, like I'd been, before I was real, before I was a man. They didn't matter a thought, it wasn't like they were human.

"Do not be too proud, man." It was the Ship again. *"We had them restrained, they were retarded, set not to use their weapons. Not in use, a risk of too much damage . . ."* I just looked around and laughed right out. I was feeling like that, tired suddenly and a little mad.

"Yes . . ." It was the Boy. The Boy again . . . the real one, the naked one. I whirled and he was shouting for me, he was somewhere up towards the middle of the Gallery. "Don't think you're clever, Candy Man! You've still got me to consider!"

I moved a bit and then I could see him. He was up by the Henge and his pistol was pointing too far to the right of me.

"Just because you think you've learned to kill . . . Candy. They were only Androids . . . Candy . . . ?" It certainly figured, it was how it had to be. The Ship made them when it needed them from the patterns it had, it was economic, machine-like.

The Boy stood close up against the flat side of one of the standing stones. He held his pistol out, his flesh was light against that rock. He was fifty yards off and it'd have been no good to speak to him.

I slowly levelled my weapon. I felt tired, unclean, leaden, uncaring. I was still Android enough to feel that somehow it was wrong to have to kill him. But I had to go on. The Boy was in my way. If he got me the race would be lost, he had to go.

When I pressed the plate I didn't care any more. I wasn't an Android, it really dawned on me right then that I could do what I liked. I fired and kept on firing as he slid down the great stone.

I went over that way. I had a feeling that I ought to feel bad about it. That Teacher was the only man I'd killed before and I found I didn't care about that either now. All down the stone you could see white deep stars where the charges had gone through him as he fell. He lay untidy looking at the bottom. I had done that, decided and done it—the pistol felt dirty and very heavy so I dropped it on the floor. I really needed my gloves then, when I wanted them they weren't there.

When the weapon was gone I felt better. It was all over now, it was finished. Now the Boy was dead the way to the galaxies was open, he hadn't died for nothing. I'd had to kill him, now the race would be the way it ought to be. I cheered myself like that, but I knew it was bad and it was all wrong.

"YOU KILLED HIM!" K—it was K and I'd forgotten her!

She came and crouched over the Boy. Bent over him, then whirled up her head to stare hate at me. I saw tears on her cheeks. She'd loved him all the time and despised me. How could I hope to understand what they did?

I stood where I was. The sun was setting over the stones and broken instruments. I looked deep into her eyes and there was only hate there and she was still the only beautiful thing I'd seen. Round her neck, resting on one tear wet, perfect breast, she was wearing the Toroid ring.

That vital thing, the clue to the Matter Engine, the symbol and talisman of all our new hope and she wore it for a trinket!

I let my shoulders drop. It was too much. Hell, maybe she was right. The whole future of our race, the greatest Artifact and a trinket on her chest. I looked up and it was still a trinket when you compared it to the Galaxy, set it against the Milky Way. I don't know how long I stood there. Then suddenly she reached out and snatched the Boy's pistol.

Her mouth came open. I saw the small, perfect teeth. She laughed when she saw my pistol on the floor. She didn't say anything, she was hardly breathing. I backed off and the weapon came up to point at me.

"You killed him . . ." She got up. The Toroid fell inside her blouse. Her thumbs worked on the pistol control. The muzzle opened like a flower as she screwed up the power.

I turned and ran. Even then I didn't want to hurt her. I was frightened, sure, but I still wouldn't have hurt her. She stopped laughing and then came slowly after me.

I scrambled and slipped through the smoking instruments. She burned a couple of charges into the floor behind me. She was laughing again and she sounded like she was mad. I don't think she tried to hit me. She wasn't in any hurry, she didn't have to be. Very soon I came to where the seamless glass of the cupola arched up out of the floor.

There wasn't any way out. I ran left. It was hard to

breathe. Maybe I was crying, it was hard to see as I slithered along that crystal glass with the stars and cold space out there. I drove my bending man's legs on and on, away from the stalking Girl.

I kept looking back and she was always twenty yards away, walking along the edge of the instruments. Just walking there, the pistol in both hands, walking inside me, easily keeping up with my panic run around the great circle, laughing at me. Maybe that was when I really learned what it was like to be a man.

Then I fell over a Boy I'd shot. There were three of them there. I remembered it like day. They'd tried to get around me and I'd killed them very carefully because I didn't want to knock any holes in the cupola.

I got up and slipped down again in the blood. I held up my hand and looked there. It was red and it was sticky. The truth came like a kick from a horse. They'd been real . . . they'd been men! There were no connections in the spilled brains of the first one . . . they'd been human!"

"Oh, yes . . ." The Fat Man was there too. Standing very still in his immaculate uniform. "They were the human ones—the Ship regenerated them in flesh and blood—as they were a few hundred years ago. They already existed as Androids—those two you know. They were the Androids. Anyway, it's always quicker and cheaper for the Ship to make men . . .

"Almost real . . . almost human . . . not quite. Fooled you?"

I turned and the Girl was very close. She'd stopped laughing. Even the way I'd known her, you wouldn't have known what she was. Hell, she fooled Wolf too!

She brought up that terrible pistol and aimed it square at me. She was just five feet off.

She fired, but she fired it wrong. Jerked the plate instead of squeezing it off. The charge went straight over my head. There was a great crash back there somewhere. The blast knocked me down and we were showered with broken crystal. The Ship screamed.

I looked up at the Girl. It was like being hypnotised. She frowned, then spread her legs for better aim. She edged a little closer and brought the weapon down for another try.

"No . . ." sighed the Fat Man. He waved at the Girl. She froze, the pistol half down, her mouth half open and wet looking. We stood still and left off shouting.

"Only an Android . . ." went on the Fat Man. "We can't have her blowing holes into space, letting all the air out. I'm not sure the Ship can repair itself any more . . ." He seemed to see me, he smiled. "I can't have her killing you, much as I might enjoy it. There are only the three of us left now . . ." The Girl tottered and fell on to her back. She lay there, just as she'd stood, the pistol pointing stiffly into the air. My stomach went to ice.

"Just you and me and the Potter. We're the only three Corps men left; you wouldn't know she was an Android, would you? She was a woman I knew once. She was based on the Ship as you were based on the Earth's Deep Machine, you couldn't be expected to know her . . ."

He helped me up and then forgot me. He went on talking as if I wasn't there. Maybe he was making excuses, but I didn't think he was. I thought he was just talking and that he was mad.

"Even though I love her like myself I can't let her kill the last man but two. I loved them both, you know, her and her brother.

"That *Potter*, that Potter, he says I just adapted them for my pleasures, used them like puppets, lived through them . . . made them do the things I wouldn't do for myself. Oh, yes, I knew what they did . . . enjoyed their pleasures, helped them do the things I wanted, the things you can't do by yourself. You do see? You have to have someone to do what you can't for yourself. Why should I deny myself anything? The last man but two?

"That Potter, he says maybe I didn't know what I was doing, that it was just sub . . . subconscious, but all the things they did, that was what I really wanted. He says they did the things for me that I was ashamed of; they weren't real, he says, they were a fiction so I could make them do everything. But that Potter, he doesn't realise. I *enjoyed* what they did. I used to lie back and enjoy what they did, they were real enough for me . . ." He looked up at me suddenly, half grinned. "He says making pots is better, but I don't believe in perfect shapes, do you? I don't believe in beauty, I don't believe in right and wrong. I don't believe in doing anything you don't know the reason for, I just believe in what I *enjoy* . . ." About then I tried to prize that pistol out of the Girl's hand, but I couldn't move it so I just stood there and listened to him.

"Just we two left—the fag end of the race—it didn't seem to matter what we do, it doesn't matter at all, not really. All the rest, the ones that are in the records, stored inside the Ship, they don't care to be alive any more, they don't care to be men, they'd rather be part of the machine, we're the only ones that want to be human." He looked quickly around, wiped the palms of his hands across the belly of his uniform. "That's what *I* think—the Potter says they're all dead, that the mechanisms never worked properly, that the ship lost most of them somehow, that most of the Ships were lost anyway. He says there may be other Corps men in other parts of the Galaxy, but he's mad, that Potter, all he thinks about are shapes. But really they're all hiding in the Machines, they don't care any more, it doesn't matter what I do, anything as long as it's interesting, gets me to the next day . . ."

"What about K? What about *her*?" It was like talking to a record that kept slipping, half the time I didn't understand what he was on about; but I wanted to know about the Girl . . . I wanted to know what he'd done to her.

"I loved them," he said. "How I loved those two . . . K, her brother. She was my daughter, that Girl, I set the program for a son, but, you see, we were in a high light fraction, something went wrong. There was a lot of that. When the bottle opened she was a girl, and she wasn't right, before she died I had the Machine take her in. Then, when it didn't matter any more, the Good Ship made her into an Android for me, how she should have been. Fifteen, fifteen years old, as she is now. The same process as yourself, modified, because she should have been a boy it made the Boy too, her identical twin, except for the sex. They loved each other too, you know . . ." He smiled, like he was remembering some nice childish antic. "Perhaps it'd be better to say they loved themselves. I brought them together with my mind, found games for them to enjoy. A wonderful time, all thanks to the Good Machine . . ."

"You could use it like that? The Ship let you do that?"

"There was only me left then, the Potter came later in another Ship. He didn't care, all he cares about are shapes . . . I think . . ." He looked around quickly, then whispered. "I think he's a little *mad* . . ." He paused again, looked at me out of the corner of his eyes, a sort of fear was in them. "Me . . . *me* . . . you don't think I might be a little . . . a *little* mad too?"

He was splendid in that uniform, there wasn't one of his grey hairs out of place. He looked *good*, in a way I hoped I might look like that one day, but I was glad he went on talking and I didn't have to answer him.

"Oh, yes . . . I loved them . . . gave them everything I wanted . . ." He stopped talking to take another look at me, it was different, his eyes were even brighter, it was as if he was seeing me for the first time since he'd started talking.

"I loved you too, you know . . ." I stopped breathing, I don't know what I thought in that moment. "I knew you all the time, of course . . . like K . . . I knew you, but you couldn't know me. I was sad you didn't know me . . ." His brow creased, he looked at me like something was my fault.

"So tell me . . . ?" I didn't know what he meant, but there was something there, something important. There was something about him that got right in me and twisted there.

"When I was a young man I was you. I volunteered to watch the Earth's Deep Engine. The me that is you wanted to escape the Corps, escape the way things were going . . . thought perhaps things would improve on Earth when the Machine ran it, but I'm not optimistic now . . . are you?

"I am you. I couldn't let her kill you, not even my

181

own daughter. I couldn't let her kill myself. Did you think I was mad? You were mad to think those peasants on Earth were the race's best hope. I know better now, I'm older than you. I don't hate you for it, I was younger then, perhaps I was a little mad. You don't think you are *mad*!" He stopped again, pressed his hands to his temples. My head ached too, it was pretty hard to understand.

"You don't *think* you're a little mad?" The Fat Man was still talking, he was mad, and I was pretty confused myself. "I made her like her mother . . . I had the Ship make her just like her mother . . . I thought you'd like that. You don't think I'm mad? I had a lot of fun that you didn't!"

I turned away. It was the fag end of the race all right. I didn't believe a word of it, but I couldn't think of any other way it could have been.

I kept telling myself how he wasn't her father—how I wasn't her father—not in any biological sense like we have on Earth, I mean. He just picked the egg and provided the fertilisation, that's all, he'd just selected the patterns, that was all. The Machines had done most of it. And I wasn't him, not any more. I was me before him, before I went bad. Anyway, I told myself, hell! What the hell, it didn't matter. I was myself! Whatever the patterns, the genes, however he was begotten, a man was *himself*—and that was the end of it!

Cold wind from somewhere hit the back of my neck. I'd been so interested I hadn't felt it before. I turned from the man that might have been me and looked through the shattered edges of the cupola. The Girl's last charge had gone through there and the stars were broken away.

Some of them, just near the impact, they were still lit. Some flickered there, the cracks in the crystal spread across them. Another morning sun streamed in there, dimming the sunset on the other side.

It was just one more illusion. Only a projection of the lying Ship. I could see the real surface out there. Trees and a square cut ocean a few miles off. It was the top of the Earth, you could see snow-capped mountains poking

182

up through the layers. When you stepped down two feet you'd set foot on soft grass, wet looking, with dew on it, lush where the rain washed down off the Ship.

The Ship wasn't in space, it wasn't half-way to the moon . . . maybe the Corps hadn't ever left the system, maybe they'd never left Earth. Maybe they'd just made images like they had, men could sure fool each other well enough, it'd be just one more false layer in this world of lies.

On the grass I looked back to the Fat Man.

"What about the Matter Engine? Will you make the new Ships? Will the Corps try for the galaxies?"

"A model . . . I'm making a model of it. To scale! It'll show the Artifact well enough . . ." It was what I'd guessed. Nothing would come of it. I stepped out further on to the solid earth.

CHAPTER TWENTY

WHEN I WAS outside I could finish it from there. I could do the last part of my Purpose. That concrete, I was going to finish it, I was going to send it all away. I could un-make it.

All that was necessary was to stop *holding* it, to stop thinking of it so it would go away. I hadn't told the Fat Man about it, or maybe he knew and didn't care.

Concrete wasn't quite as good as the real thing, you had to *keep* it in existence, you had to keep remembering if you wanted it to stay. Or the Machines had to— that's what the thing on my back was for. When I stopped holding it all in my head the layers and the cities just dissolved and the concrete went back to where it came from.

I let it down gently. Took a week over it. Everybody just ended sitting on the surface and wondering what had happened. Some people were over the Seas and they had to swim for it, but most of the water followed the Old Seas so there weren't so many that got wet. The most violent thing was when the nutrient reservoirs broke and that stuff went gushing down what was left of the Streets. It could have been bad when the music went, but that faded slowly and when it finally stopped the people hardly noticed.

When it was all over the pink thing fell off my back and the connections dropped away. I didn't need the power of the Deep Machines any more, not those big vibrations, nobody did.

All that was twenty years back. It's been a time of starting again, of planting and working. Small societies, village communities you'd have to say, modest but healthy. The sea came up some, but we found the first surface— the one that was made before the Matter Engines— we found we could live on that; farm on it and live in the top rooms. When the Earth lost the mass of the concrete it moved further out from the sun. Somewhere near its real orbit, I suppose. Anyway, the ice caps are building again and the water is going down slowly. When the concrete pillars and Streets went, just that dropped the level thirty feet. It'll be like it was one day.

The second generation is running things now. They haven't had their brains burned at any Rites, so my job is about finished. It'll be all right, they're natural men and women, just growing things and living. They didn't have any truck with Teachers. The population is going up, there must be twenty millions of us all over the world.

There are Teachers about even now, sad behind their lead faces. There's nothing for them, all they know about is the past, past excellences, academic things.

Now that I'm free I go sometimes to a high place and look down. You can see the Ship from where I go. Half in the sea it is, settling there in the shallows. It's badly corroded; stained with salt and draped with seaweed. A wreck with white metal rot climbing its great flanks, thin metal peeling back to show the structure there. Maybe, when we're ready, if it lasts, maybe it'll give us the clues to build more Ships and reach into space the way we're meant to.

Sometimes, when it's evening and that first bright star comes out, sometimes I wonder what happened to that Saver we were always dreaming about. I think about what I've done and how things have changed and wonder if it was me all the time. But really, I know I'm not. I still don't believe in Luck either.

For a long time I wore that bandage over my eyes and pretended I was blind—to myself, as much as anything. Like a punishment for the trouble I'd caused, for who I was, for ending the world. Then one day I saw the Fat Man through the hole in the Ship's cupola. He was in there, the man I might have been, and he was looking back at me. He shook his head and turned back to the instruments and I watched him scurry from one to the other. I wondered what he thought he saw in them, what illusions the Ship was feeding him. Like the World and the concrete, it was only what you thought it was, what he saw was just as real to him. I threw away the bandage and I haven't worn it since. I've never wanted gloves again—and I find I don't care about mirrors.

I still sometimes see him, doing the same sort of things. He has the Girl with him sometimes and that isn't so funny. K . . . I suppose the Fat Man switched her on again, brought her back.

Once or twice I thought she saw me. She didn't make any sign, she didn't seem to want to kill me. It's all different from what it was at the time, of course—but I still call her K to myself. I still can't speak the memory of her name. I suppose I ought to be still afraid of the Boy, but I've never seen him again.

I've seen the Potter. He waved to me, but he went right on digging his clay. Wolf came back too, I don't know how he got out of the Ship . . . he'd get out of anything!

"It's good having a robot dog. He protects me and he's happy to belong to me. Dogs make good robots . . . or robots make good dogs. When the sun shines he comes down with me to some village or other and I spin up some floss. I stand in the shade and remember the Matter Engine, think of when I was an Android, of what we've won and what we've lost.

One thing more—that floss I make—I don't put anything in it, it's not necessary these days! Anyway, it's all for the kids. They still call me Candy Man, they don't fear me these days, not at all—and I don't fear myself either.

A Selection of Crime Thrillers from Sphere

A Selection of Popular Fiction from Sphere

A Selection of Biography from Sphere

A Selection of History and Archaeology Titles from Sphere

A Selection of Science Fiction from Sphere